Monseigneur d' Hulst

A Martyr of our own Times

Life of Rev. Just de Bretenières

Monseigneur d' Hulst

A Martyr of our own Times
Life of Rev. Just de Bretenières

ISBN/EAN: 9783337058142

Printed in Europe, USA, Canada, Australia, Japan

Cover: Foto ©Raphael Reischuk / pixelio.de

More available books at **www.hansebooks.com**

J. M. de Bretenières
Miss. ap. en Corée

A Martyr of Our Own Times.

LIFE OF

Rev. JUST DE BRETENIÈRES,

Missionary Apostolic, Martyred in Corea in 1866.

From the French of

RIGHT REV. MGR. D'HULST,

RECTOR OF THE CATHOLIC INSTITUTE OF PARIS.

EDITED BY

VERY REV. J. R. SLATTERY, A

RECTOR OF ST. JOSEPH'S SEMINARY, BA

———

NEW YORK, CINCINNATI, CHICAGO:

BENZIGER BROTHERS,

Printers to the Holy Apostolic See.

1892.

THE excellent letters of the author of this Life, Mgr. D'Hulst of the Catholic Institute of France, and of His Eminence, Cardinal Gibbons, say so well and so much better than I can the lesson conveyed by the life of "A Martyr of Our Own Times," that it is only needful to direct the reader's attention to them.

May this little work prove the germ of a fruitful growth of the missionary spirit among our American youth.

J. R. S.

TO

St. Joseph,

THE FIRST MISSIONER,

WHO, IN THE FLIGHT, BROUGHT

OUR LORD TO AFRICA,

THIS LIFE OF

A MARTYR OF OUR OWN TIMES

IS HUMBLY INSCRIBED.

J. R. S.

LETTER FROM HIS EMINENCE JAMES CARDINAL GIBBONS.

CARDINAL'S RESIDENCE, 408 NORTH CHARLES STREET,
BALTIMORE, January 17, 1891.

MY DEAR FATHER SLATTERY:

I am much pleased to learn that you have had translated into English and are preparing for publication Mgr. D'Hulst's admirable Life of " A Martyr of Our Own Times."

There is no virtue more needed by young aspirants for the ministry, especially by those who are destined for self-denying missionary labors, such as await the students under your charge, than a thorough spirit of self-sacrifice. Without this interior spirit the most exacting and severe exterior discipline is but a delusion and a snare, and is in danger of being cast aside as soon as the young levites are removed from the vigilant eye of their superiors.

This virtue of self-control, so earnestly inculcated by Our Saviour, seems to have been the characteristic trait of Father Just de Bretenières, which was consummated and consecrated by a glorious martyrdom.

God grant that the perusal of this volume may inspire the candidates for the sacred ministry with the spirit of self-sacrifice, which will purchase for them that interior liberty by which Christ has made us free!

I am yours faithfully in Christ,

JAMES CARD. GIBBONS,
Archbishop of Baltimore.

vii

LETTER FROM THE AUTHOR.

The Catholic Institute, Paris, 74, Rue de Vaugirard,
Paris, August 10, 1890, Feast of St. Lawrence.

VERY REVEREND RECTOR:

The labors consequent upon the ending of the scholastic year have prevented my replying sooner to your welcome letter of June 6th, transmitted to me through Rt. Rev. Bishop Keane of the Catholic University of Washington.

I am truly confused at your eulogistic appreciation of the little biography, the Life of Just de Bretenières, which modest work has no merit save that of being a sincere tribute to the memory of a holy life followed by a holy death.

I am greatly pleased to think that, translated into English, this simple narration may help enkindle in the hearts of American youths preparing for the priesthood the fires of the apostolic spirit.

Your American Church is the fruit of the apostolate of old Europe. Hence it is but just that, having attained the degree of prosperity and moral power which we now behold with admiration, she should, in turn, bear her tribute to a more distant apostolate. Heretofore this young Church has been absorbed, as it were, in the work of her own increase and growth, finding in the immensity of the territories of American civilization ample sphere for the display of her zeal.

Now, however, that the Catholic hierarchy is firmly established throughout the extent of the vast continent upon which you live, why should you not cross the Pacific as did your fathers the Atlantic, and join upon Asia's ancient soil your European brethren, uniting your labors to theirs, and with them struggling,

viii

and finally triumphing by patience, by prayer, by word, and by works, over the obstinate resistance these ancient peoples oppose to the Gospel?

Very consoling amid the many sad spectacles which darken the horizon of France is that of the honored rank our dear country still holds among the foremost of the propagators of the Christian religion. Yet do not for an instant suppose that we are jealous of those who, beyond the seas, feel their hearts fired by the same supernatural ambition. *Messis multa, operarii pauci.* May you succeed in rapidly increasing the number of such who will bring to the service of the apostolate that undaunted courage, that energy, that intelligence which have made your countrymen the pioneers of modern civilization! And this new testimony which you will thus give to the vitality of the Catholic Church will be by none more joyously applauded than by your brethren in France.

It is indeed from the depths of my heart that I pray God most ardently for the development of your apostolic undertaking, the prosperity and success of St. Joseph's Seminary.

Accept, Very Reverend Rector, the assurance of my respectful devotion in Our Lord.

M. D'HULST,
Rector of the Catholic University of Paris.

AUTHOR'S PREFACE.

The biographical sketch which we present to the Christian public is a work of piety in the two acceptations of the term—piety towards God, which finds its aliment in the example of a holy life and a heroic death, and the piety of affectionate remembrance, which induced us to accept the mission that we were offered, more than ten years ago, by the venerable parents of the young martyr.

Incessantly interrupted by other labors, and resumed oftentimes only at long intervals, our task was not accomplished ere the death of M. and Mme. de Bretenières. Whilst regretting deeply that thus we could not give to their tenderness a supreme consolation, and to their generous sacrifice a first recompense, in making them witnesses of the honors accorded the memory of their holy child, we have felt more at our case, on the other hand, in revealing the fact that the son's virtue was inherited from his parents. More than one touching page of this little book had been very difficult to write under the eye of those whose eulogiums were inseparable from the narration of their actions.

Comprised within the narrow limits of an existence of twenty-eight years, twenty-six of which were spent in his own family and in the novitiate of the Missions, the life of Just de Bretenières offers nothing to attract men's attention save the glorious immolation through which he entered into rest. All the beauty of this life is within; and under penalty of travestying the reality, we must needs give our little book the character of an ascetic work. The history of the saints is that of asceticism in action; and without departing from the rules imposed upon biographers by the wisdom of the Church, without forgetting that it belongs to the Holy See alone to decide the titles and the honors of sanctity, we believe we may safely assert that the soul of Just was of the race of saints. Hence, only those will find pleasure in our pages who are interested in the work of grace in a soul, and the progress of that soul by fidelity thereto.

As the last months of Just's life were spent in the mission of Corea, and as his precious death inaugurated a long series of persecutions and catastrophes for the Church there, we have believed it our duty to give an abridged account of those circumstances and events which, in a measure, were naturally connected with the young missionary's history. All this has been recounted elsewhere, and in a more complete form than by ourselves. The historian of the Church in Corea, the biographers of Mgr. Berneux, of Mgr. Daveluy, of Mm. Beaulieu and Dorie,—Just's companions in martyrdom,—have already given such information to the public, and their narration is doubtless far superior to ours. But as a biography should suffice of itself, and as it is not to be supposed that the reader of this book should have always before him other works treating of the same events, necessity has led us, towards the end of this volume, into some historical digressions—a fault against art perhaps, but pardonable because of our desire thereby to enlighten our readers on points intimately connected with the life we are narrating.

Whilst tracing these lines, we learn that the missionaries now established in Corea have finished the apostolic process of the martyrs (Corean) of 1839, and that the *process of the Ordinary* is about to commence for the martyrs of 1866. The cause of their beatification thus enters upon its first phase, and it will end, we doubt not, by the act declaring them *venerable.* The time, then, is well chosen in which to add a portrait to the gallery of heroes illustrating the Corean Church. Moreover, the era of liberty and peace which appears, at last, to have commenced for this portion of Christianity is also propitious to the publication of our narration recalling the days of trial.

The pages of our little book, if ever they read it, will be to the children of the martyrs in that far-off land beyond the seas instruction in the school of one of their own apostles. And in our own dear France, which amid all her wanderings has never ceased to be everywhere God's grand missionary, more than one heart, we dare hope, will be thrilled at this souvenir of that tranquil heroism which had its origin in a truly Christian education, and was developed in the exercise of the most humble and most solid virtues.

M. D'HULST.

PARIS, November 1, 1888, Feast of All Saints.

CONTENTS.

LIFE OF JUST DE BRETENIÈRES.

CHAPTER I.

JUST'S CHILDHOOD AND YOUTH (1838-1859).

THE Church calls the death of her saints their birth; and
her martyrology is a perpetual defiance to death, the
day of the saint's death being ever named therein his birthday.

In adopting this heroic language of the sacred liturgy, we
state that the birthday of Just de Bretenières was March 8,
1866; for it was on this day, having joyfully laid down
his life for the Lord, he received in exchange the imperish-
able crown of eternity. And let those who have loved him
know that this is not merely a hope—it is a certainty: the
Church does not permit us to pray for her martyrs.

If we desired simply to honor him whom God has glorified, we would limit ourselves to a narration of the circumstances of this second birth. But we seek especially the
instruction of those who read these pages; and we feel assured that they will find it in the history of this life, of
which martyrdom was, in a measure, but the natural crown.
It is a touching story, which discloses to our gaze a chain
of divine graces and the progress of human fidelity in the
path of perfection, through its firm hold upon this chain.
To render this biography attractive to the fervent Christian, there is no need of detailing all the circumstances of

its environment. Under the tranquil exterior of a life conformable to the ordinary conditions, the interior life has its struggles and phases, visible, whilst the combat lasts, only to the eye of God. But when the hour of triumph has sounded for the soldier of Christ, they who are still battling on the same field have a right to ask the happy conqueror for the secret of his victory. Therefore we essay this account of our martyr's life.

Simon Marie Antoine Just Ranfer de Bretenières was born at Châlons on the Saône, February 28, 1838, in a mansion situated in the Rue Saint George, which has since become the office of the sub-prefecture. At that time it belonged to Mme. de Bretenières' father, the Baron de Montcoy.

Providence seems to have surrounded the cradle of this child with every salutary influence, every honorable memory, every incentive to virtue. His maternal grandfather, whom we have just mentioned, was distinguished for his valor in the defence of Lyons against the revolutionary armies in 1793. Taken prisoner, he delivered himself by a prodigy of audacity and physical strength.[1] Made prisoner a second time, he was reserved for the guillotine; but some mistake as to the names delayed his execution, and the 29th of July brought him liberty.

Just's paternal grandfather, M. Ranfer de Montceau, Baron de Bretenières, had also experienced the hardships of the revolutionary period, but in another way. Emigrating to Switzerland, he remained there only a short time, his taste for the fine arts soon attracting him to Italy, where he made a living by the exercise of his talents. He even obtained a professorship in the Academy of Florence.

On his return to France, he courageously applied himself to the study and practice of law. The government of

---

[1] Taken away on foot between two officers of the law, he knocked one off his horse, and killed the other, after disarming him. This was not known at the time of his second arrest, or he would have been shot immediately.

the Restoration discerning his merit, and acknowledging his fidelity, appointed him first president of the Court of Appeals at Dijon, his native place.

His son, Baron Edmond de Bretenières, inherited his father's taste for the fine arts. After an arduous course of study in the classics and law, he followed the path marked out for him by his father, devoting to travels and to painting the first years of his youth; he returned to Dijon to enter the magistracy, a career soon interrupted by the Revolution of 1830. A short time before the latter event, he had married Mlle. Anne Marie Lantin de Montcoy. The first child born of this union died soon after its baptism; and its pious parents waited nearly seven years for a new pledge of the divine benediction. At last, in the month of February, 1838, after they had been married eight years and a half, during a sojourn at the house of M. de Montcoy, the birth of a fine, healthy son realized their most ardent wishes, and changed their prayers into thanksgivings.

The infant was baptized on the day of its birth, in the church of St. Peter at Châlon, by the curé of that parish, the Rev. Vivant Compain, its grandfather, M. de Bretenières, and its maternal grandmother, Mme. de Montcoy, standing sponsors.

We shall not yield to the common temptation which leads certain biographers to discern much that is remarkable, indeed most marvellous, in the life they attempt to portray. We have no hesitation in acknowledging that Just's childhood and youth were spent in a manner conformable to the ordinary conditions, if we may truthfully thus style the austere simplicity of a family wholly regulated by the spirit of Christianity. Those blessed, holy homes where the vivacity of reciprocal affection alone tempers the severity of duty, where the parents withdraw from the world, in a measure, the better to devote themselves to their children's education; where everything—occupation, residence, intercourse—is regulated solely with a view to this work; where religion enlightens the conscience and conscience reigns over all,—such homes were numerous among the nobility of our provinces, and the higher class of citizens of our cities, both before, and for some time after, the French Revolution. But in our day, alas! they are rare; and when we see generations springing up that will soon make homes of their own, we cannot forbear asking if these examples of Christian firesides are to disappear forever. We scarcely dare say, though it is easy for all to foresee, what is to become of education, and consequently of the nation, when luxury, frivolity, the spirit of display, precocious ambition, cupidity, the spirit of insubordination and disrespect, succeed in their continued encroachments upon the family. Meanwhile, the evil grows day by day, and threatens French society with complete dissolution. Hence it is a salutary and patriotic work to recall Christian parents to a sense of their duties, by directing their attention to models of their state of life, of homes which their own should resemble—contemporary models, for which reason, no one, in advance, can declare them inimitable. Consequently, it will not be useless to give a brief description of the domestic circle in which Providence cast the future missionary's early days.

His father, having retired from public life, spent his time in the management of his private affairs, the cultivation of the fine arts, and in good works. The winters were passed partly at the abode of M. de Montcoy in Châlon, partly in Dijon, in an old mansion situated on the Rue Vannerie—a handsome, secluded dwelling amid court-yards and gardens, in the rear abutting on ancient ramparts, whence one has an extended view over the country. It

was a solitude in the centre of the city. The Château de
Bretenières, some leagues from Dijon, was the summer residence. In these different places of sojourn the family
life was uniform,—always filled with the same duties. To
pray, to read, to paint, to manage their property, to attend
closely to their children's studies, to associate themselves with
all the charitable works of the country, to undertake and
carry to completion the construction of several churches in
the suburbs of Dijon,—such were the occupations of Just's
parents, during the whole period of his childhood and
youth.

We are not of the number of those who compare the moral
life to the solution of an equation. We do not believe
that mere statement of the terms gives us a possession of
that secret which can be solved only by the free will.
Many others have happily found in their own family both
example and protection, similar to that which encom-
passed Just de Bretenières on his entrance into life. And
yet how many of these have not squandered that inherit-
ance of honor and virtue! This is a mystery of moral
liberty. But be the possible abuse of this what it may, it is
none the less the duty of those having charge of souls to provide them every protection against evil, every incentive to
good. Such advantages were not wanting to Just. In the
serene, vivifying atmosphere which we have just described,
his strong, healthy nature developed readily, as if in anticipation of the work of grace.

In the month of April, 1840, a little more than two
years after Just's birth, God gave his parents a second son,
whom they named Christian. This new pledge of benediction proved to the elder brother a source of much that
was beneficial. Closely pursuing the same studies and en-
joying his sports in the companionship of a brother so near
his own age, Just had no need of seeking outside the fam-

ily either for that incentive to study which is found in
emulation, or for the necessary distractions and recreations
of youth; and nothing prevented their parents from devoting themselves entirely to their holy charge, in concen-
trating at their own fireside all the anxiety, all the resources
incident to the work of education.

Whilst yet a very little child Just was remarkable for
his thoughtfulness and great self control.   Full of affection for his grandfather, he knew how to moderate, for his
sake, the petulance of childhood; and at a sign from his
mother this child, only three and a half years old, would
immediately stop playing, to stand silently turning the
leaves of a book placed on a desk before the aged man, or
to tenderly wipe his face suffused with perspiration, which
was one of the effects of a painful malady.

His mother's affection has preserved the remembrance of
the following incident, referable to this period of his life,
which would be scarce worth relating, did not the course of
events permit us to regard it as the sign of a precocious
call of grace. A priest having called to see Just's parents,
little Just took hold of the bottom of the visitor's cassock,
and said to him, " If I am good, when I grow up, will you
give me a dress like this? "

Just's childhood was signalized by a very remarkable oc-
currence, the precise character of which we do not intend
to state, although it seems difficult indeed not to recognize
therein the hand of God. It took place in 1844, when
Just was six years old and his brother four. The two
children, under the supervision of a governess, were playing
together in the garden at Bretenières, digging the ground
with sticks, when suddenly Just stopped.   " Be quiet," he
said to his little brother, and looked down into the hole
he had just dug. " I see the Chinese! I see the Chinese! "
he now exclaimed. " Come, let us dig deeper, and we

shall soon reach them." Christian, peering into the hole, declared that he saw nothing. Just insisted upon the reality of the sight, and, whilst digging vigorously, described the appearance of the Chinese and their costumes. Bending over the hole again, he declared that he could even hear their voices. Christian, filled with astonishment, made no reply, and the two children soon resumed their play.

But this extraordinary event was not effaced from their memory. They never spoke of it to each other again, nor did either of them mention it to their parents. Twenty years afterwards, however, Just told the story to one of his fellow-students of the Seminary of the Missions. One day, when they had gone to the Institution of St. Nicolas of Issy, to visit a child ten years of age, whom Just had placed there, the latter questioned his little protegé concerning his tastes and his desires for the future. The child replied that he wished to be a missionary. And as Just's companion seemed much surprised at this, from one so young, especially as the little one spoke very earnestly, Just said, " I am not at all surprised; my own vocation dates back even to more tender years than his. Long before I was his age, I knew that I was to be a missionary." And hereupon he narrated in detail the scene in the garden. He afterwards again related this curious incident to another aspirant of the Seminary of the Missions, M. Wallays, now Superior of the College of Penang. It was the eve of his departure for Corea. In a conversation full of tender feeling, in which he made known to his friend the principal circumstances of his life, to excite within his heart lively sentiments of gratitude for the great things God had done for him, he reproduced the history of this singular event, the living image of which, in his memory, not even twenty years of silence had dimmed.

Nor did his brother retain a less vivid remembrance of
it, and our account is taken from his own words. Some
additional particulars we find in a letter written after
Just's death by one of his cousins, who had the story at
second hand. According to her, as Just insisted that he saw
and heard the Chinese, and Christian neither saw nor
heard anything, they called their mother. But her testimony corresponded with Christian's. Just then said to
them both in a tone of great earnestness, "You cannot
hear them, but I do very distinctly. There they are,
mamma, far, very far off, at the bottom of this hole, on the
other side. They are calling me, and I must go save them."

We note another indication of his precocious vocation in a
remark which he made to his brother, just about this time,
when not more than six or seven years old. The two were
talking together at the Château de Bretenières, to which
place they were both much attached. "When you own
this property," said the younger brother, "will I have to
leave it?"— "Oh, no!" replied Just, "do not worry about
that. It will never belong to me, for I am going to be a
priest, and it will be yours."

These are the only especial incidents of which we find
mention among the souvenirs of his childhood. Yet all
who knew him then unite in declaring that even before his
First Communion he was remarked for his precocious virtues
—an angelic purity, the spirit of piety, an obedience invariable and founded upon love for God. Of a reflective cast
of mind, he understood and appreciated the education,
serious and indeed austere, given him by his parents. A
person who instructed Just in music when he was about
eleven or twelve years old, quotes the following remark
which the child once made to him, at that time: "What
is often the result of an education when not conducted like
ours? Idleness, a life content with smoking cigars."

The virtue of this child consisted, then, in the faithful performance before God of his allotted duties—a foundation the surest and best, without which we know virtue is rare in childhood. Yet prevenient grace already drew this chosen soul to the highest desires, murmuring to it the sweet invitation, *Amice, ascende superius:* "Beloved one, go higher." The pious mother was accustomed to give her sons spiritual readings, which she took great pains to explain to them. One day, losing sight of their tender years, she spoke to them of perfection. Some time after, she overheard the following dialogue: "Tell me, Just," asked Christian, "what perfection is. I did not altogether understand mamma's meaning when she was speaking to us about it the other day."—"Perfection, I think," replied Just, "is like a high mountain, very high. It costs us much time and labor to reach the top; but there is no need for discouragement; we can always get there, *if we wish.*"

The intellectual like the religious education began early for the two brothers. A foreign governess taught them to speak and write German quite as well as they did French, which they were studying at the same time. Foreseeing that later classical studies would interfere with a more profound culture of the German, M. de Bretenières determined to profit by their extreme youth in grounding them solidly in this language; and in the spring of 1845, when Just was not more than seven years old, the family went to reside for some months at Kissingen, in Bavaria. Here a young priest of the diocese of Würzburg was tutor to the children. The following year they made another sojourn at Kissingen, whence they went to Bamberg, where Just and his brother attended a public school. The Archbishop of Bamberg permitted a young priest of his diocese to accompany the family to France. This priest, just ordained, was very pious. Utterly ignorant of French, he taught entirely

in German. The religious instruction of his pupils seemed
to be his especial care and pleasure. Already penetrated
with respect for the priesthood, Just was delighted to have
for his teacher a man so filled with the spirit of grace. One
day he asked his mother if all priests were not saints. On
her replying that being men they were fallible, a proof of
which was Judas, who betrayed Our Lord, although all the
other apostles were saints, glorified by martyrdom, Just
said, "Well, I believe M. W. is a saint, for when he explains
the Catechism to us, I see his face light up, an aureola appears around his head, just like you see in the pictures of
saints. Isn't it so, Christian?" The latter declaring that
he had seen nothing at all, Just said nothing further on the
subject.

A French tutor succeeded the German priest, and continued with his pupils until they made their First Communion, which was on the 12th of September, 1850. Just,
who had been kept back, waiting for his brother, was twelve
and a half years old, when the two, accompanied by their
cousin, A. de V., in the parish church of Montcoy, received
Our Lord for the first time. That same day, in the chapel
of the château, they renewed their baptismal vows, and consecrated themselves to the Blessed Virgin, each child lay-
ing at the feet of her statue a petition expressing his heart's
dearest desires. What was Just's petition? No one knows,
for he did not say, and the three notes were burned without
being read by any one save the writer. But considering the
astonishing precocity and constancy of the holy desires
that germinated so early in this young soul, and led him
to martyrdom, we may readily believe that on this day
the Blessed Virgin was made the confidante of the most
generous of oblations.

The First Communion made, a more arduous course of
study must now be entered upon. Their tutor's health not

allowing him to continue his work, the parents were called upon to decide a most important question—whether to go on with their children's education at home, a plan so suitable to their tender years, or have recourse to public education, better adapted to develop the spirit of emulation and to form the character by contact with others. But by the side of these advantages of a college, that world in miniature, what are not the dangers, and what the risks in exposing innocent souls thereto! Just's parents did not hesitate long. Wishing to keep pure and unsullied for God the treasures which He had given them, they charged another ecclesiastic to instruct their sons in the classics at home, reserving to themselves the lessons in German, the accomplishments, and religious instruction. As to education properly so called, they assumed the entire direction, for this purpose detaching themselves more than ever from all other cares, withdrawing, as it were, from the world, and transforming their house into a veritable college, or, if you will, a sort of monastery. An inflexible regularity presided over the employment of time, the studies and classes succeeding one another in invariable order. The children's sports were natural and spontaneous, deriving all their interest from the gayety, the earnestness, the agility, the reciprocal affection of the two. To prevent all pre-occupation of the toilet, their dress was simple and uniform, a loose blouse fastened at the waist by a sash constituting their style of dress in all seasons, until the end of their studies.

The vacations, though interrupting their work, made no change in the simplicity of their mode of life. Always careful to protect his children from whatever might awaken in them a taste for luxury and develop an eagerness and unwholesome desire for pleasure, M. de Bretenières allowed them little or no acquaintance with the amusements and distractions of the world, and relied upon travelling to sup-

ply the necessary relaxation of mind and body. Even here
we find the imprint of that austerity characteristic of this
virile education. Their journeys were made on foot, a sack
on the back, the geologist's hammer in the hand. The father
and mother took part in these fatiguing excursions, which
lasted one or two months. For nine years they spent the
vacations in this manner, during that time climbing the
greater part of the mountains, and traversing nearly all the
valleys, of Switzerland, Savoy, and the Vosges. Adventures
were not wanting to the little party, and the fireside conversations on the return to France were frequently en-
livened by such recollections. We here insert an account
of the most remarkable of these, although it took place
long after the epoch of which we are now writing, and
when Just had passed a year at the Seminary of Issy. It
is quoted from a letter which Just wrote to his former preceptor on the 28th of September, 1860. The reader
cannot but observe therein that vein of frank gayety which
was one of the charms of Just's character.

"Without preamble," he writes, " I copy for you an
extract from *The Gazette of the Upper Rhine,* a journal
issued three times a week at Belfort, which you probably
do not receive.

" 'Day before yesterday, Saturday, September 22, were
arrested in the railway station of our town the supposed
perpetrators of the sacrilegious robbery committed last
Thursday in the church of Fresse-en-Comté. They
hoped and sought to escape justice by fleeing to Switzerland. They are even more strongly suspected of the assas-
sination committed some time ago on the road from Paris
to Mulhouse. These individuals are three in number.
The one styling himself the father is of medium height;
his hair and beard are white and short; he is apparently
from fifty-five to sixty years old, and possessed of great

shrewdness and energy. The second in years is tall and slender. He had doubtless stolen his clothing to disguise himself, for his jacket was short, and did not look as if it had been made for him. The third,[1] whom we suppose to be the youngest, was in ecclesiastical costume, but also disguised, as one saw at a glance, for his cassock was so much too long for him that he was obliged to hold it up to prevent its dragging on the ground. They had with them hammers, chisels notched on the edge, and other instruments which bore witness against them. They made no resistance to being arrested, but feigning complete ignorance of any cause therefor, asked repeatedly of what they were accused, protesting that it was all the result of a mistake. Taken in charge by five policemen, they were conducted through the town, surrounded by a great crowd of people first to the police office, next to the examining magistrate, and thence to the court of justice. Thoroughly searching their persons, the officers found each one armed with a dagger. After all three had been closely questioned, the pretended father asked to be put in telegraphic communication with the mayor of Dijon, by whom he professed to be well known, adding that himself and several of his relatives had belonged to the magistracy of that place.

" ' As the warrant of arrest and the description are issued from the bar of Lure, it is there the case must be tried. The day being now too far advanced to admit of their starting at once, the police were about to conduct them to jail, when the examining magistrate, out of respect for the habit which the youngest of the three wore, decided that it would be sufficient for the officers to keep guard over them at one of the hotels. Two policemen guarded them, never leaving their chamber an instant

[1] Just, although older, looked younger than his brother.

during the whole night. The next day, Sunday, the accused asked not to be taken to Lure on foot, or by the public stage, but by the cars, they offering to pay their expenses. This request was complied with, and accompanied by two officers, they were conveyed to the station and put in a car. Reaching Lure, they were received by the whole brigade of police, who with difficulty cleared a passage for them through the dense crowd, collected at the depot, all eager to behold the perpetrators of crimes so horrible. Thence they were immediately taken to court. Our Lure correspondent has not yet informed us of the result of the trial. We shall make it known to our readers in the subsequent numbers of our journal.'

"These numbers may be dispensed with," adds Just, "when I tell you that the undersigned, who was one of the three prisoners, has been released; also his two accomplices, the mistake having been discovered."

In the above graphic account all is true, except the statement that it was quoted from a newspaper. Just's next letter revealed the pleasant artifice. "I am sure," he writes, "that you must have laughed heartily over our misadventure, as I intended you should; however, it is now time to tell you that I am ignorant of the existence of a *Gazette of the Upper Rhine*, the article being the production of my own pen."

The epilogue of this little story is not less curious than the portion of it we have just read. The parish priest of Fresse took advantage of his sermon at Mass to join his anathemas to the maledictions of the populace against the supposed robbers. When the identity of these latter had been established, Cardinal Matthiew, who entertained the highest regard and esteem for the De Bretenières family, sent the hasty pastor a letter of censure, ordering him to make public reparation from the pulpit.

Just afterwards acknowledged to one of his fellow-students at the Seminary of the Missions that, in spite of the comic side of this adventure, he had really suffered to see the holy habit which he wore dishonored; although, at the same time, he felt true joy in thus making an apprenticeship to insults and bad treatment.

But let us return to Just's boyhood and the vacation tours. These hardy walkers gleaned far more than pleasant souvenirs for memory's store-house. Early initiated in the natural sciences, they took advantage of these excursions to enrich their collection of rocks, minerals, fossils, insects, and birds, which collection was, during the whole year, the object of their incessant care. Later on, to increase their knowledge, they visited museums and cabinets of natural history, and corresponded with scientific men, acquiring thereby a wonderful amount of information in this branch of study. The scientist, M. Charles d' Orbigny, who had initiated them in geology, said one day that he could teach them nothing more about the nature of rocks; and he had them both received members of the Geological Society of France, not wishing to leave to another the pleasant duty of sponsorship herein.

Of the two brothers, Just seemed to take the more pleasure in these instructive distractions from study, and his interest in his collections appeared spontaneous and deep; yet, as was afterwards learned, this was with him rather a matter of conscience and precocious wisdom. Comprehending his parents' desires, he had entered into their designs, and sought to encourage in his brother a taste for such diversions, as he well knew would prove serviceable in various ways. One day, when Just's vocation, now clearly defined, betokened his early departure from home, his preceptor, seeing him apparently absorbed in his rocks and his birds, said, in order to try him, " And what if you

have to leave all this?"—"Oh! that would not be hard
to do," was the answer. "Do you not see that I occupy
myself thus mostly on account of my father and my brother?
It interests them so much now; and it will be even more
interesting to them when I am gone." We perceive that
later on, when from the seminary, which he had then entered, Just continued to direct, by letters and words of
counsel, his brother's course of life, yet undecided, he still
expressed great interest in these collections for the purpose of exciting Christian's interest therein, constantly rec-
ommending them to his care, and thus seizing the opportunity of mingling with technical instruction exhortations
to piety.

The vacation tours had another charm for Just, known
to himself alone: he found them the occasion of disciplin-
ing himself in advance to the rough life of a missionary.
This vocation, which he still kept a secret, was henceforth
ever before his mind. To brave cold and heat, fatigue and
thirst, was for him to enter upon an apprenticeship in the
life of an apostle. Hence he was never seen to sit down
when they halted, to drink in passing fountains, to lighten
his clothing under a burning sun, or to increase it on
entering a cold valley. Likewise, in the geological harvest-
field, which was abundant, he always got hold of the heaviest
stones, and gayly carried the weightiest sack. Equally in-
genious in seeking labor and in avoiding pleasure, he rarely
took the gun (excusing himself on the ground of his near-
sightedness) when he and his brother went gunning for
birds to enrich their ornithological collection, reserving
to himself the task of carrying the game and stuffing the
victims. Yet, when he did shoot, on exceptional occasions,
his address appeared in this as in everything else.

To the study of the classics the two brothers added that
of the living languages. We have already seen how, at a

very early age, they had been initiated into the German
tongue. This they continued, conversing therein under
their parents' supervision ; and they also acquired a considerable knowledge of English. Music and painting
they also studied, Just applying himself to these latter
rather from obedience than inclination. His musical knowledge he found of great service in the Seminary of Issy,
where he was given charge of the organ. There he applied
himself most successfully to the accompaniment of plain
chant, according to a method taught him by the learned and
holy Abbé Leclerc, too soon, alas! snatched by death's re-
lentless hand from the Society of St. Sulpice. This duty,
in which the science of harmony ruled, pleased his serious
nature and developed within him a taste for music. Perceiving this growing attraction, he mistrusted it, and soon
relinquished the satisfaction. Thus, contrary to the usual
conduct of young people, whose ordinary incentives to action
are amusement or caprice, Just was guided in everything
solely by duty and the spirit of sacrifice, which inspired him
to embrace or to quit occupations, even as pleasure gen-
erally influences others therein.

Had he ever yielded to those passions surging in all
youthful hearts ? The testimony of his tutor, who was
constantly with him for seven long years, gives us the highest idea of his virtue. He was of a nervous, sensitive temperament, and in his early childhood manifested exceeding
sensitiveness to pain. "The least suffering overcame him,"
said his mother ; "even the cold wind flushing his cheeks
would make him cry." But from the age of twelve years
he sought to harden himself, and the spirit of mortification
henceforth appeared in all the details of his life—in his
avoiding overmuch indulgence in eating, in his promptly
shaking off sleep, in his disdain of the toilet, in his efforts
to forget self, always giving the first place to Christian, and

assuming the least agreeable tasks himself.   The tutor we
have mentioned says that during the seven years Just was
under his care he never knew the boy to be guilty of more
than two or three pranks, two or three manifestations of
selfishness, of self-indulgence, or of ill humor.   The following is an example of one of these.   The children had learned
a game of cards in which they took great pleasure.   For
several consecutive days they thus amused themselves after
dinner, when finally something occasioned their pleasant
pastime to be deferred.   Just complained of this, not deem-
ing the reason for such deprivation sufficient ; and to punish
him for his impatience, they were forbidden to play the
game for several days.   It was not resumed, and no one
ever alluded to it again.   That a trifling imperfection
like this should appear worth mentioning certainly shows
that this holy child had accustomed his parents and teachers to expect from him wonderful equanimity of temper.

    We hesitate to place among his faults the first and last
falsehood which he ever uttered, for in this case he was the
victim of another's mistake.   This child so pure was accused
one day by a person who had charge of him of a very
grave fault.   He was perfectly innocent, and did not even
comprehend the accusation.   The accuser, however, thinking very differently, insisted upon an acknowledgment ; and
to escape the severe alternative that threatened his refusal,
Just yielded.   The additional wrong was inflicted upon him
of exacting the promise that he would not mention the oc-
currence to his mother.   Ten years afterwards, when at the
Seminary of the Missions, Just still bewailed this weakness,
and told his mother that he could not forgive himself for
having lied, and also concealed anything from her, although
it had been with a good intention.

    These testimonies of rare virtue dispense us from noticing
some of those traits of character which would have been ob-

servable in an ordinary child—his recollection in prayer,
his taste for the ceremonials of worship, his pleasure in
serving at holy Mass and in ornamenting the shrines on Cor-
pus Christi, his tender devotion to the Blessed Virgin, etc.
One distinctive mark of his piety was zeal. Not satisfied
with loving God himself, he longed to inspire others with
that same love; and whilst yet a small child he used to
urge his brother thereto, and preach little sermons to him,
the latter in his simplicity hearing them then without surprise, but at a later day remembering with wonder and admiration, as he recognized therein the precocious grace of
the apostolate accorded this chosen one. As the sight of a
holy, fervent priest thrilled Just's heart with joy, equally
so was he saddened on meeting one careless and lukewarm.
" Oh ! how can this priest be so lacking in zeal !" he would
say in accents of the deepest sorrow.

Thus passed the years of his childhood and youth. Towards the end of the year 1856, at the age of eighteen, he
went to Lyons to undergo an examination for the degree of
Bachelor of Arts. A little confusion and lack of self-pos-
session having caused him to fail, his virtue shone conspic-
uous in the composure with which he accepted his loss—
a loss soon repaired, however, by a brilliant examination,
in which he enjoyed the additional pleasure of having
Christian a companion in his success. All his spare moments were now devoted to a most laborious study of German. Whilst making himself master of its classical
literature, he went back to the beginnings of the language
and studied its primitive poets. This was the period when
with Christian's assistance he translated a work on *Christian Art,* in two volumes, by Dr. Neumayer. This occasioned a correspondence between the translators and the
author, and the following year the two young people made
the latter a visit at Freiburg in Brisgau. He was much sur-

prised at their proficiency in German, as well as at the maturity of their understanding, their philological, historical, and philosophical knowledge, of which the elder especially gave ample proof in his ordinary conversations and his inquiries.

Just, having now finished his studies, expressed no preference for any profession, and the subject was not mentioned to him, for every one, his brother alone excepted, surmised what was passing in his soul. Towards the autumn of the year 1857, by the advice of his director, he informed his parents of his long cherished intention of quitting the world. He wished to put it into execution without delay and to receive the ecclesiastical habit at once. M. and Mme. de Bretenières were not of the number of those Christians who honor the priesthood, yet shrink from the idea of giving their own children to God in this holy state. One consideration alone, and that worthy of their great faith, withheld the word of consent from their lips, and urged them to ask of Just a delay of two years. He had great influence over his brother; and had not that brother, only seventeen years old, and much less matured than the elder, especial need, just at this time, of Just's example and counsel? M. and Mme. de Bretenières thought so ; and Just complied with their request, saying nothing more for a while about his vocation. During the two years promised he was the most devoted friend to his brother, and the most vigilant, fortifying counsel by example, and obtaining Christian's compliance with all that he desired of him, through the twofold reliance of the latter upon Just's virtue and affection. He prepared with Christian for the examination for a university degree, although he had no idea of undergoing the examination, and his arduous studies herein were merely to fix his brother's attention on the work.

It was during this period, in the year 1858, that M. de Bretenières took his two sons to Frankfort, where he had the pleasure of presenting them to the Count de Chambord. Just, ordinarily so little in unison with worldly ceremonial, manifested on this occasion neither timidity nor awkwardness. Outward expression with him was indicative of the reality ; and as he had ever piously guarded in his heart those traditions of fidelity and respect which his ancestors so cherished, he consequently found himself at ease in the manifestation of such sentiments. His habitual placidity gave place to enthusiasm when he had the happiness of thus approaching the Prince who to him was the representative of all that he revered ; and on his return he frequently expressed his regret at not having had an occasion of proving his devotion.

The end of the promised two years approached. The autumn of 1859 was spent in excursions through the valley of the Grisons. Just broke the silence anew, and told his parents it was now time for him to follow his vocation, that he was already twenty-one years old, and quite ignorant of certain branches of study necessary to the priest. He met with no resistance. And now arose the question, What was his precise vocation ?

Just thought it the religious life in the Order of St. Dominic : the religious life, because from his tenderest years he had been enraptured with the evangelical councils ; but why the Order of St. Dominic? This was the only one with which he had any acquaintance ; for, at this epoch, other religious were seldom seen at Dijon ; the neighborhood of Flavigny attracted attention by reason of Father Lacordaire's work; and during Just's childhood he had several times met the illustrious Restorer of the Friar Preachers. One day the latter had said to Mme. de Bretenières on her showing him her two sons, " You must give us one."

Another time, requested by the pious mother to bless them, he declined, but pressing Just to his heart, he said in a whisper, "This one is already blessed." All these circumstances naturally exercised some influence, if not on Just's vocation, at least on the particular form which it at first assumed in his mind. But the dominating feature of his vocation was the desire, the passion I may indeed call it, for the apostolic life; and knowing that the Dominicans had missions in the Orient, he had hoped on entering the Order to be sent there; indeed, his fixed intention, as we have since learned, was to request this. However, he said nothing yet on this point, and expressed merely his desire of entering the Order.

Joining here, as in all things else, wisdom to the spirit of sacrifice, his parents feared that such a choice was not sufficiently disengaged from human influence; and as his director shared their doubts, it was decided that Just should go to Paris, to consult a guide wholly disinterested. He was sent to M. Carrière, Superior General of the Sulpicians, who advised a sojourn of at least a year at the Seminary of Issy, during which time Just could study and mature his plans. This decision was painful to the pious young man; yet with his usual docility he acquiesced, and joyfully prepared to go thither.

His brother, still ignorant of Just's determination, must now be told. Just told him one evening during a walk which they took to the gates of Dijon. Christian made no reply, and the darkness prevented his betraying by countenance the pain which this communication caused him; but his subdued manner, and the few words that he afterwards said to his mother on the subject, told plainly how great a sacrifice it exacted of him.

This announcement, although unexpected, could hardly be said to have surprised him who from the hour of his birth had been ever with **Just.** That precocious gravity, that gentleness, that manner of acting so different from other children's ways, all of which Christian had hitherto ascribed to a certain originality, now appeared to him in their real significance. " Light," he writes in his notes, " suddenly broke in upon me regarding my brother's life, which I had never before clearly understood, and I had not a shadow of doubt as to the solidity of his vocation. I recognized so clearly in his past life God's call on the one hand, and, on the other, such faithful, continual correspondence to grace, that instead of diverting him from a course that must needs deprive me of my best friend, I could not forbear giving him all possible encouragement."

Their fraternal tenderness was charming, and made their last weeks passed together at home appear very short. Their separation was delayed by the necessary preparations for the departure of the whole family from Bretenières, the parents having decided to establish themselves in Paris. for the purpose of affording their younger son the opportunity of pursuing advanced studies, and of being, at the same time, where he could profit by his elder brother's counsels.

This beautiful family life now approached its end. For Just and those so dear to him there was opening an era of sacrifices, succeeding one another up to the supreme immolation.

CHAPTER II.

THE SEMINARY AT ISSY (1859-1861).

THE 19th of November, 1859, marks an era not only in Just's life, but in that of his biographer; for it is the day on which they first met, the day on which the

biographer's personal recollections begin to blend with those
carefully treasured by others, of which, up to this time, he
has been merely the interpreter.

The Seminary of Philosophy at Issy, under the direction
of the Society of St. Sulpice, re-opens annually on the 5th
of October.   Delayed at Dijon by the circumstances we have
mentioned, Just found this pious community actively engaged in study and prayer.   It was the vigil of the principal feast of the house, the Presentation of the Blessed
Virgin, a day of great joy among the sons and disciples of
Olier.   Such of them as are in Holy Orders then renew the
consecration which separated them from the world, repeat-
ing at the foot of the altar those words which a celebrated
apostate[1] once pronounced there with them, words which
he has since sadly parodied, under pretence of guarding and
ennobling the reason—*Dominus pars hæreditatis meæ*,
"The Lord is henceforth my heritage."

Still wearing the secular dress, Just regarded with holy
envy those favored ones whom maturer years had enabled
to precede him into the sanctuary.   And among those who
here declared the Lord their only heritage, how many had as
much right as he to appropriate these words to themselves?

The writer of these lines can never forget the impression
made upon him by his first meeting with the future martyr.
Just's tall, commanding figure plainly indicated health and
strength; his energetic temperament was visible in the exceeding pallor of his countenance; his high forehead
enframed by his wavy hair gave expression to nobility of
character; his mouth, a little too large, detracted somewhat
from the charm of his features; but his eyes, mild and gentle,
beamed with the light of courage, and his glance, candid
and modest, inspired confidence at once.

The edifice in which our new candidate took his first steps

---

[1] Renan, *Souvenirs d'enfance et de jeunesse.*

towards the priesthood has been so often described that it
is unnecessary for us to do so. At this epoch the ancient
summer retreat of Marguerite of Valois had not yet seen
those vast modern constructions which now abut on the sides
of its old walls. Then, as to-day, one beheld in the low
halls, the tarnished gilding and partly effaced paintings of
its ceilings that mingling of elegance and poverty which rejoices the artist without assuring the comfort of the inmate.
To this contrast, as we have just said, had not yet been
added that of those two large buildings which, in the pride
of their towering height, seem to look down upon the old
dwelling with disdain, as if about to bid it adieu.[1]

As to the park which rises gradually to the elevated ter-
races of the *Solitude,* extending on a level as far as the
hedge surrounding the sanctuary of *Lorette,* it still guards
and preserves, with the memories of Tronson, Fénelon, and
Bossuet, the austere and charming aspect of these beautiful
spots, witnesses for two centuries of so many hidden efforts,
secret virtues, unknown prayers.

Issy is the true novitiate of the ecclesiastical life. The
reputation of St. Sulpice attracts thither those recruits too
seldom found in our day in families of easy circumstances—
mature men, who amid the activity and bustle of worldly
life realize the nothingness and vanity of all earthly things.
Mingling with the more numerous quota of youth who, with
a less marked vocation, leave the preparatory college for the
seminary, these older aspirants to the priesthood conform to
the sweet requirements of humility and of childlike docility
there imposed upon all by the practice of evangelical sim-

[1] The reader will understand that here we speak merely from an æsthetic point of
view. Those in charge of youth have great pre-occupations and duties. The insufficient space, and wearing out of some portions of the edifice, rendered additional buildings necessary; and, moreover, among the children of St. Sulpice there is
not one who does not feel grateful to the eminent Superior, to whom the Holy Father
has recently accorded a magnificent testimonial, for having provided in so ample
and worthy a manner for the present and future of clerical education.

plicity; whilst, at the same time, they unconsciously re-act
by the authority of their example upon the youthful
spirits around them, prone rather to follow the current than
to reach their end by strong personal effort. Thus the wisdom of some is imbued with frankness, and the frankness of
others enriched with virility; and this fraternal interchange
adds one more charm to the memories of this blessed spot,
which abide through life with all who have ever sojourned
within its walls.

Just was not of a nature to resist such influences: he
gave himself up to them entirely, happy in what he received, ignorant of all that he brought, penetrated with respect not only for his teachers, but also for the least of his
fellow-students, and having no idea of the ascendancy he
obtained from the first over all who approached him. The
testimony of his contemporaries on this point is unanimous;
and those who speak most admiringly of him are, at the
same time, the best, the most pious, and they who were
most intimate with him.

How shall we describe the employment of his time at
the seminary? For this it will suffice to read over the
rules of St. Sulpice, adding after each article, "Just
observed it perfectly." Silence, punctuality, application
to prayer and to study, fraternal charity, obedience, self-
denial concealed under gayety,—behold what constitutes the
ideal of a young ecclesiastic: and this is the portrait of Just.
Raising himself at the beginning above natural sympathies
and antipathies, that shoal of community life, he loved all
as his brethren and had but two kinds of preferences—the
one for the less perfect and the less agreeable, in order to
advance their welfare; the other, for the most fervent and
most edifying, that he might sanctify himself by the influence of their society.

At first life at the seminary struck him with surprise,

or, I was going to say, as a deception: he deemed it too
much in accordance with nature, too easy. His home education having been one of austere simplicity and manliness,
already habituated to the exercise of self-control and sacrifice, he expected on entering the seminary to find there the
penances of the cloister; and in this he was disappointed.
He discovered however, by degrees, that fidelity to the
rule, in spirit and detail, afforded ample opportunity for
immolation of self, and instead of regretting the absence
of imposed mortifications, he learned how to mortify himself in secret.

The work here is full of attractions for serious minds;
but the continuity of effort, the aridity of the subjects, the
severe simplicity of the scholastic forms, the multiplicity
of exercises minutely apportioning each moment of study,
and thus ever sacrificing to the requirements of rule, interest
in research begun—all these are more than enough to infuse
into the hours of study either disgust or the spirit of renunciation, according as the spirit is wrapt in itself or in God.
Just profited thereby, and in the inexperience of his zeal
even went beyond those bounds which so many others fail
to reach. Whilst laboring assiduously to regain what his
delayed entrance had caused him to lose, and striving to
keep ever in the foremost ranks of his fellow-students, he
believed it a duty of charity to give lessons in German to
one of the professors who had asked this favor of him.
Such arduous efforts, joined to the work of forming his
spiritual character, which he pursued most energetically,
and the anxiety of that great interior deliberation for which
he had come hither, and the solution of which would shape
his course henceforth through life, were too much for him;
he began to give way under them, and his superiors found it
necessary to send him back to his parents for a few weeks'
rest. Christian was delighted at this enforced leisure which

again made Just the companion of his labors, and resolved
to turn it to account. However, Just was soon able to return to the seminary, and there devote himself to the
double task which wholly absorbed him—his sanctification
and the examination of his vocation.

Before giving an account of the means by which he came
to a decision regarding this second portion of his work, let
us take a brief glance at some traits of character and incidents, showing how he acquitted himself of the first.

Just was fully convinced that so far he had done nothing
for God. Having heard one day in a spiritual reading these
words of a celebrated Sulpician of the seventeenth century,
the Abbé de Lantages, "Compared to the saints we are
devout only in appearance," "Yes, that is indeed true!" he
exclaimed, " we have done nothing. It is now time for us
to begin in earnest."

This explains the holy avidity with which he sought the
society of the most fervent and edifying seminarians. No
one of these had more of his confidence perhaps than he
of whom we now speak—a fellow-student whose premature
death permits us to disclose the secret which his humility
had imposed upon us, Father Guérin, a native of the city
of Lyons. He died in the Society of Jesus ere his admis-
sion to the priesthood. Soon after graduating from the Central School, with the diploma of civil engineer, he retired from the world, and came to Issy for the same purpose
that had brought Just hither—quest of that quietude and
freedom of mind so necessary for the solution of the great
problem of his vocation. Whilst already resolved to enroll
himself among the soldiers of St. Ignatius, the events following close upon Castelfidardo caused him to join another army temporarily, and offer his blood in defence of
the Holy See ere devoting his life to the service of the
Church. With this end in view, he left Issy in the month

of February, 1861, during Just's second year there; but the few short months which they passed together under this holy roof had sufficed to cement their friendship into an indissoluble union, rendered thus by the same ardor of faith in both, the same thirst for immolation, the same aspirations for martyrdom.

Let us listen to Father Guérin's account to Mme. de Bretenières, after Just's glorious death, of some incidents of their intimacy.

" We were both transiently at Issy," he says, "awaiting the hour marked out for us by Providence to enter, he, the Seminary of Foreign Missions, I, the Society of Jesus. Long before mutually communicating our intentions, each had divined the other's secret and our conversations disclosed it.

" We were speaking one day of the Blessed Sacrament and lamenting that it occupied so small a place in the life of Christians. 'It is really incomprehensible,' we remarked, 'man's ingratitude in refusing such a Friend anything. To gaze upon a consecrated host, listen to its divine appeal urging us to the conquest of souls in distant lands, and to remain deaf thereto, how can it be possible!' At these thoughts we were both overcome by emotion, and it was necessary for us to break off our conversation before the usual hour, or rather, to finish it at the feet of Him to Whom one may lay bare his heart. A few minutes after I met Just on the stairs: his face was radiant with joy, his eyes full of tears. 'Oh! thanks, thanks,' he said to me; 'how much good our conversation this evening has done me!'"

Thus was exercised upon this generous soul, either by God's direct action or that of His instruments, the attraction for sacrifice. Thus also was daily advanced that great affair which had led it hither.

We have said that on entering the seminary there were **two** dominant thoughts in Just's mind, the one avowed, the other secret—the Dominican life and the Missions, closely united to each other. The first of these only gave form to the second. Was there really in the circumstances shaping his vocation thus, more of human, natural influences than divine? At the beginning Just did not think so, but to re-assure his guides he consented to examine the grounds of his vocation.

As he proceeded in this examination, the doubts expressed gradually grew stronger and stronger in his own mind, until, at last, they were transformed into a certainty, just the opposite of his first views. One thing alone appeared to him to embrace God's will concerning himself—the foreign apostolate. And was this assured him, and promptly, were he to enter a religious order established in France? By no means. The religious by his very profession renounces all right to the selection of his duties. Hence the Seminary of Foreign Missions seemed manifestly the path marked out for him by Providence to follow a vocation daily growing more clear and decisive.

These interior deliberations, known only to his director, occupied the whole of his first year at Issy. It was towards the end of this scholastic year, on the Ember Saturday of Whitsun week, June 2, 1860, that he received tonsure, in the church of St. Sulpice, at the hands of Cardinal Morlot. A violent attack of rheumatism, confining him to his bed during the preparatory retreat, threatened to deprive him of the happiness of being united thus with his fellow-students in this, the first step towards the priesthood. But on the very morning of the ordination a sudden amelioration of the disease permitted him to join them; and every one remarked the ardent joy, the angelic recollection of the new aspirant during all this long and solemn ceremony.

Six weeks afterwards the vacations began, furnishing Just the opportunity of showing the fruits of that interior work to which he had devoted the past year. Notwithstanding his deep affection for his parents and his brother, he felt like an exile out of the seminary, although keeping the rule most sedulously by a faithful discharge of all its practices of piety, and endeavoring to preserve all those advantages resulting from a continued correspondence with the most edifying of his fellow-students.

His parents took him to the waters of Plombières for the purpose of recruiting his health, now somewhat impaired, and it was at the end of the season here, that M. de Bretenières and his sons made that excursion into the Vosges, in the course of which happened the misadventure already narrated.

Re-entering the seminary in October, 1860, Just joyfully resumed the exercises of the community life. The bonds of intimacy between the Abbé Guérin and himself were drawn more closely than ever. On the departure of the latter for Rome to be enrolled in the pontifical army, Just succeeded him in charge of the infirmary. Very mortified himself, and little attentive ordinarily to the details of the material life, Just had not much natural aptitude for these functions; but charity proved to him an able instructor, and he was soon quite proficient in the gentle art of condescending to the needs and desires of the sick. His zeal here found full scope in an employment bringing him so closely in contact with many of his brethren and permitting him to add weight, by his delicate attentions, to the counsels and the example of virtue which he gave them.

From the commencement of this second year his choice was fixed in favor of the Seminary of Foreign Missions. However, by the advice of his director, his resolution was kept secret for a while, the better to mature it; and he communicated this knowledge only to his parents and his old preceptor, and even then, not as yet positively settled, although

a letter to the latter, dated February 21, 1861, reveals the
ardor of his attachment to this generous purpose. He writes:

"I tell you, but in confidence, that I have turned seriously
to the Seminary of the Missions. Say nothing about
it just now, because I am not yet positively determined
on this point, and shall not be for three or four months;
also because when I do decide I intend mentioning it to no
one outside our small family circle, ere executing my
designs, by this means avoiding the questioning and
close observation that would surely follow, for I well know
what will be said. Whereas, my decision once made, nothing,
no one, can shake it. Father and mother, to whom I have
already spoken, will not oppose it. Believing it the will of
God, I shall not disturb myself as to the manner of its ac-
complishment, knowing that all will be brought about in
His own good time."

By May his decision was irrevocable, and the moment
had now come for him to inform his parents. He did so one
day, whilst paying them a visit in the apartments which
they had rented in the Rue de l'Est, opposite the *École des
Mines.*

The interview was a sad one. M. de Bretenières saw
thus vanish the hope which he had still nourished of rec-
onciling the rights of paternal love with the exigencies of
that zeal which transported his child. Embracing at a
glance the meed of suffering in store for himself and those
dearest to him—the separation, most probably forever in this
world, the hard life of a missionary, and perhaps death
amid tortures for Just—the father could scarce bear up
under his weight of anguish.

Not less affected, but more sustained by grace in this trying
hour, Mme. de Bretenières proved herself a worthy companion of those heroic mothers whom history associates in
the martyrs' glory, by their sublime acceptance of the sac-

rifice of their children. **Praying** silently whilst Just was unfolding his plans, she obtained from God the strength to thank Him for having chosen her offspring for the honor of such an apostolate.

After the disclosure followed some moments of silence. Just, although calm apparently, suffered internally a violent struggle. Expecting strong objections, desperate resistance, he had prepared himself in advance for this encounter, and he was armed for the strife. Seeing that his parents made no reply, he thought they were meditating their plan of defence, and that it would be well for him to begin the attack. In a few words he recalled all those motives which rendered his vocation sure, all the precautions taken to prove it, all the concessions made to defer the decision. Would it not be great presumption to question the will of God when so clearly manifested? His father and mother still made no reply. More and more disconcerted by their silence, Just was afraid of yielding, and under the influence of this fear he let his feelings carry him too far. "Nothing," said he, "can now make me change my resolution. I know a student of the Seminary of Foreign Missions, who being unable to obtain his parents' consent, in just such a case as my own, and fearing they would use strong measures against him, left secretly for pagan lands, after only a few months' sojourn at the seminary."

This implied suspicion was an injustice to M. and Mme. de Bretenières, who had certainly afforded no grounds for it, or merited that such precautions be taken against them, and it wounded them; for although the thought of Just's plan had pierced their hearts, they had raised no objections to it, comprehending truly that they were face to face with an irresistible vocation. However, they did not reproach their son, who, at a later day, reproached himself for his words.

And shall they dare condemn him who have never known what it is to impose such sacrifices, for love of God, on those whom one loves, nor to do violence to themselves, lest their holy resolutions be shaken by the tears of a father, the mute grief of a mother!

On the very day of this disclosure, May 15, 1861, M. de Bretenières took his son to the Seminary of the Missions, and presented him to the Superior, at that time the venerable M. Albrand. The will of God was generously accepted herein by all whom it immolated.

Just had now not more than two months to pass at Issy. With that composure so characteristic of his courage, he returned to Issy, and applied himself to his ordinary duties, his preparation for the examination in philosophy, and his office of infirmarian, as if nothing of importance to him had taken place. Was it not to please God that he desired to become a missionary? And in what better way could he do God's good pleasure now than in the perfect performance of each day's tasks?

On the 15th of July, 1861, Just bade adieu to the Seminary of Issy. Let us here note especially the words of the worthy Superior of the house, Just's spiritual father also, during his stay there, written after his martyrdom, to Mme. de Bretenières—a summary of her holy child's two years' sojourn in that seminary. "My recollections of this period," he writes, "are all embalmed in the perfume of his virtue, but it offers few incidents.

"Calm and uniform, his life was a beautiful, attractive one, without noise, without show. The following is the notice I found of him in our register: 'De Bretenières, Just, from November 19, 1859, to July 15, 1861: was for two years the edification of the seminary by his piety, and our delight for his gentleness and agreeability. His good qualities, perfected by an excellent education received wholly in his family, prepared him for great things.' In writing these last words," continues M. Maréchal, " I did not comprehend them, and often after thought of changing them, as not in accord with the painful and obscure occupations of a missionary. To-day, their meaning being now plain to me, I leave them just as they are."

Before entering the Seminary of the Rue du Bac, Just wished to satisfy his devotion to the Blessed Virgin by a journey to La Salette. He made it in company with the writer of these lines; and the two friends passed five days together in this solitary spot where the austere beauties of nature proclaim to man God's grandeur, and Mary's tears invite the Christian to penance and reparation. The hours fled rapidly and agreeably, spent in the long prayers of the Church, at the stations scattered along the fountain, and in those endless conversations wherein their mutual effusions of piety and friendship seemed to melt their two souls into one, thus, by a union stronger than ever, defying, as it were, the impending separation. O souvenirs ineffable, the brightness of which twenty-eight years have not been able to dim in the memory of him who then began to assist in the powerful transformations of grace in the heart of his generous friend, in whose heroic death but a few years later he recognized the crowning of a life which was holy even then!

At the end of their sojourn at La Salette, the two pilgrims were joined by Just's brother, who had just passed a successful examination in Lyons for his degree in letters. He came hither to thank the Blessed Virgin for his success, and to enjoy once more the society of a brother from whom he was soon to be separated, by the exigencies of Just's holy and austere vocation. On their return the two brothers stopped some days at Dijon, thence proceeding to Paris, where their parents awaited them. But Just did not repair to the paternal mansion. He had promised his parents to give them some weeks of this year's vacation; but longing to take his place in the family of missionaries, he determined to put himself under obedience to his new Superior, and to make acquaintance with his new brethren, ere fulfilling this promise.

Hence on the 25th of July, 1861, he entered the Seminary of the Rue du Bac, where he was received with fraternal cordiality. His pleasure, though great, was at first not unmixed with surprise; for the aspect of this zealous community differed sensibly in many respects from that of the one he had just quitted, where multiplied observances of discipline and scrupulous regularity in the order of exercises were deemed essential in developing the untried virtue of its inexperienced inmates. Here, however, were souls already tempered by trial, for no one had so far entered the novitiate of the Foreign Missions without having reached it through the path of sacrifices. Greater freedom in their way of living, more fraternal familiarity, something of hardihood and roughness, or rather off-handedness in their manners,—all this would strike one at first. It required but a short time, however, to discover under this envelope great solidity of virtue, a spirit of profound recollection and deep charity, great zeal for evangelical perfection, and an energetic determination to conquer self.

Just was too well versed in spiritual matters to remain long under a misapprehension arising from mere difference of appearances. A few months after his entrance here, he wrote as follows to his former preceptor: "I was under the impression at first that I had entered a society whose members took life easy, just as it comes, and where there was not much interior work; but this impression proved a greatly mistaken one. I soon understood that a house from which men are to go forth trained to war against

Satan, and thoroughly armed for conquest, must needs be
the object of God's most abundant graces. Such is indeed
the case in this house; and if you come here this winter,
I shall tell you some things which may indeed astonish you,
and which prove that the race of saints is far from being
extinct."

During this, the early part of his sojourn in the Rue du
Bac, Just's superiors permitted him to go out nearly every
day, to see his family, or to make geological excursions
with his brother on the outskirts of Paris. It was vacation, and the venerable M. Albrand hoped by this indulgence
to Just to afford some consolation to the bruised hearts of
the parents who had so generously given their child to God.
Towards the end of August, these latter returned to the
Château de Bretenières, accompanied by Just. This was to
be his last visit to the scenes of his childhood, for according to the rule of the Seminary of the Missions students
were not allowed to pass the vacation out of the house
which the community owned at Meudon. So much was
Just master of himself, that his exterior betrayed not the least
emotion on this occasion; yet a letter to one of his friends,
written on the eve of his departure for his old home, and in
great moderation of language, leaves one to conjecture what
a combat was going on in his soul. "I shall have especial
need of your prayers," he writes, "during the few days I am
going to spend in Bourgogne, for many things will there ar-
ray themselves against me. No matter how great the soul's
joy in sacrificing all to God, human nature is always there,
its voice is always heard. Help me by your prayers to
overcome herein, that I may begin to enter upon the road
of perfect detachment and abandonment." And elsewhere,
referring to his parents, he says, "I really prefer to return
here in about ten or twelve days, but my desires are held in
check by the thought that I ought to give a little more of my

vacation to my parents. I would rather a thousand times
have to combat their opposition, but I meet with none;
yet I see that my father is wearing away in silent grief,
and my mother is overwhelmed, whilst my brother frankly
tells me of his sufferings. God's grace sustains me under
all this, but it is none the less painful to me to feel that I
am the cause of so much suffering to others. Live Jesus!
Is it not sufficient recompense to know that I am following
God's will? Pray for my parents."

During the three weeks of his sojourn in Bourgogne,
Just concealed from his family the anguish that pierced
his heart. Wishing above all things to avoid keeping their
feelings on edge, and thereby sapping their courage, he
resumed his former occupations with tranquil simplicity,
arranging his collection of minerals, and stuffing birds, at
the same time giving his brother and his father a thousand
suggestions regarding the continuance of their geological
works and the compilation of the notes taken in their last
excursions. He probably never displayed so much interest
as he did now in these scientific pastimes which once occupied his leisure, and which he hoped might prove a sol-
acing diversion to the dear ones he was about to leave.
But even all this failed to dissipate the cloud of sadness
hovering over the household; and sometimes his very
cheerfulness, in striking contrast to the grief depicted on
his parents' faces, increased the intensity of their feelings.
Conversation languished, and the preparations for the separation went on in the midst of silence and stifled tears.
Just wished to see for a last time all that he was going to
sacrifice—the friends of his early days, the old servants of
the house, the church at Châlon where he had been baptized, that of Montcoy where he had made his First Communion, the cemetery where his grandparents slept their
last sleep. **The day of departure arrived.** The whole

family left the Château de Bretenières in profound silence. On passing out of the village, Just, crushing an emotion for the first time visible, murmured these words, "At last it is accomplished!" He immediately regained his composure, and quietly accompanied his parents to the old hotel of Dijon. On the morning of the 19th of September he went with them to the sanctuary of Fontaine-lès-Dijon, erected upon the site of the chateau where St. Bernard was born.[1] His brother, who heard Mass here with him, noticed that the day's Gospel[2] contained these words of Our Lord, "And every one that hath left house, or brethren, or sisters, or father, or mother, or wife, or children, or lands for my name's sake, shall receive an hundred-fold, and shall possess life everlasting."[3] Just also noted the coincidence, but it was not until two years afterwards that he mentioned it to his brother, and what a consolation it had been to him. At an advanced hour in the evening of that same day on which he heard Mass at this shrine, Just left the paternal roof to take the cars for the seminary. To see him so tranquil and smiling one might have supposed that he was starting out on an ordinary journey; and yet he was bidding his last adieu to all earthly hopes!

[1] This venerated spot, where Louis XIII. founded a monastery of the Order of St. Bernard, was bought in 1840 by a venerable priest, M. Renault, who afterwards ceded it to M. the Abbé de Bretenières, our martyr's brother. Devotion to St. Bernard, interrupted by the Revolution, has there been restored; and the sanctuary is now served by a society of diocesan missionaries, of which society the pastor of Fontaine is a member.

[2] September 19, 1861, feast of St. Seine, a native of Burgundy and a Benedictine abbot.

[3] St. Matt. xix. 29.

CHAPTER III.

THE SEMINARY OF FOREIGN MISSIONS (1861-1864).

ON the 21st of September, 1861, Just entered the Seminary of the Rue du Bac, never again to leave it except as a priest and missionary. It was the feast of Our Lady's Seven Dolors. The young aspirant's piety rejoiced at this coincidence, which thus placed his parents' sacrifice and his own under the patronage of the great Consoler of the afflicted.

The community being still at Meudon for the closing days of vacation, Just's superior permitted him to go out nearly every day with a professor of the Seminary of Issy, an especial friend of the Bretenières family, who, having charge of the scientific course, was delighted to explore the basin of Paris in company with Just. Judging from Just's letters to his brother at this time, giving him an account of these geological excursions, one might suppose that the study of this science in which he excelled still held a high place in his affections. But other letters, written to his friends at St. Sulpice, show him already entirely detached from these intellectual pursuits, and preoccupied with them in appearance only, merely to make them a source of diversion to his parents, and lighten their grief. With this end in view, he also urged his father to make a journey in company with Christian, knowing well that his mother would find in solitude and prayer what he counselled the others to seek in the distractions of travelling. Hear how he consoles her in these first days of their separation: "I feel no inquietude," he writes, " and I have very great confidence in the Blessed Virgin, because of the impossibility of her allowing any one who has abandoned

all into her hands to fall into an abyss. I hope, dear
mother, that you have the same confidence. For is it not
indeed true that nothing engrosses your thoughts so much
as your children? And without wronging your maternal
heart, which loves us devotedly, may I not say that the
Blessed Virgin is the best of all mothers ? If it be impossible then that an earthly mother remain deaf to her child's
prayers, with what greater reason may we not believe that
the Queen of mothers, whose glory is to bestow and to bless,
will never refuse to aid her spiritual children, invoking her
as their refuge? It is true that such confidence is difficult .
to acquire, and that it demands great faith as well as great
mistrust of our own lights; yet we can at least ardently
desire it. This desire is, with God's grace, the first step
we can make therein; the fruit comes later, given us by God
as our recompense. Hence, let us ask this confidence of
Him, and He will give it."

Behold the language of faith. Had not he who now
spoke this language of consolation to his mother learned it
from her in his first infantine utterances ? Such is the
recompense of true Christian mothers.

The vacations were over; the aspirants returned to the
Rue du Bac, and went into retreat on the 5th of October.
Just hastened, after such a period of emotions and cares, to
plunge his soul in the bath of prayer. For the first time
he made a retreat according to the method of St. Ignatius.
Here there are no discourses; all passes in silence; four hours
of meditation a day take the place of sermons; the rest of
the time is spent in the examination of conscience, spiritual reading, reflection, or the pouring out of the soul
before the tabernacle, or at the feet of Our Lady's image.
They who have never followed this method know not the
wonderful resources contained therein for the development
of the spiritual life. They are frightened at the antici-

pation of those long days passed face to face with self;
they believe that if ordinarily it is very difficult for them to
spend even one hour in mental prayer, how much more so
must it be to sustain such an effort for several hours daily.
O vain apprehensions! These Exercises are for him who
makes the retreat a surer guide, a stronger support, than
all the discourses one could hear. The writer of these lines
has seen persons, who were not only strangers to piety, but
even slaves to sin, from which, however, they sought release,
courageously enter upon this path and traverse it with
equal facility and happiness. It is here, in this contact
with God, in this admirably combined series of interior acts,
that the soul is inspired with the knowledge of its end,
with a horror for sin, with the infinitely sweet grace of true
repentance, and then with the desire of following Jesus
Christ in the way which He marks out for us by the successive mysteries of His life. It is here God's designs are
revealed in the fruitful work of election. It is here the
Christian is armed for the strife, and goes forth renewed in
spirit, burning with ardor for the service of the divine King.

If these spiritual exercises produce such effects in a soul
but moderately prepared, provided it be faithful to the
grace of the moment, what fruits must they not bear in a
generous heart, long open to divine love, and already initiated into the austere joys of sacrifice? And we know
that such was the soul of Just; hence we are not surprised
at the extraordinary fervor one perceives in his correspondence after the close of this retreat.

But "fervor," says St. Ignatius, "consists rather in
acts than in sentiments and words:" *Amor debet poni
magis in operibus quam in verbis.*[1] So, too, says Our Lord
in the following text of Scripture: "He that hath my
commandments, and keepeth them, he it is that loveth Me "

---

[1] Spiritual Exercises. Meditation to obtain spiritual love.

(St. John xiv. 21).   Penetrated with this truth, our aspirant, without losing a moment, began to apply himself to
his new occupations.   Always mistrustful of self, it was
not without timidity that he entered upon the study of
theology.   The course of dogma was then taught in the Rue
du Bac by one professor; and as it embraced a period of
three years, it happened, that only once in three years
new-comers commenced at the portion which ought to have
served as their initiation.   Just encountered at the beginning perhaps the most difficult part of theology—the treat-
ise on grace, and he applied himself to it with that humble
fidelity so characteristic of him in every duty.   But even
this study, so closely connected with his vocation, although engrossing his mind, did not possess his heart.
He pursued it conscientiously, yet reserved the dearest and
strongest energies of his soul for intimacy with Jesus.

Not only practising piety himself, he counselled others
thereto, with a wisdom that knew well how to proportion
his advice to their spiritual capacity.   His correspondence
with his brother on this point is a model of what zeal for
souls can inspire.   Knowing that idleness would prove
more injurious to Christian than anything else, Just never
ceases to impel him along the path of labor, especially in
the scientific course.   He does not rest satisfied with mere
generalities in the way of advice and promptings to study ;
but he enters into the minutest details thereof, making use of
his own great knowledge of natural history for the purpose
of arranging a technical programme for his student, which
left no loop-hole for indolence and negligence even had
Christian been thus disposed.   The accuracy of his knowledge, the precision of language in which it was expressed, added weight and authority to the instructions by which the
elder brother sought to stimulate the ardor of the younger, in
the course of study mapped out for the latter.   From time to

time the accent of piety makes itself heard amid the language of science. "I forgot to say to you yesterday," Just writes, "that you must guard against losing sight of God, amidst these engrossing occupations. Do not allow yourself to be too much influenced by what is seductive, pleasing your fancy and appearing fair and right to you, without examining whether it be founded upon a principle of good. You remember, that you laughed some years ago when I spoke to you of the vanity of all things human. This, however, does not prevent my speaking to you again, and dwelling upon such an all-important subject. Yes, vanity, vanity! This is a serious matter. Do you understand it thus? Reflect often upon it. I am not reproaching you at all, I am merely giving you a little advice ; or, rather, it is Our Lord Who gives it, not I ; for frequently did He speak in this manner....Pray for me, for I have far more need of prayers than yourself."

The following year the note changes ; the study is not forgotten, but spirituality occupies a larger and ever increasing share in Just's fraternal effusions. Perceiving in his brother's soul that work of grace which will soon develop a vocation similar to his own, he discreetly and in quiet conformity with the progress of the divine action draws this soul so dear to him to an intimate knowledge of the Saviour, assisting it to foresee the value of renunciation and sacrifice. The third year Christian is at the Seminary of Issy. The future apostle now feels no restraint in speaking to him of divine love ; and he does so with transports of ardor arising at times to eloquence ; then, stopping suddenly in the midst of these effusions as if confused at his own temerity, a living lesson of humility adds strength to the burning exhortations of his heart.

Such was the solidity of Just's virtue during the first months of his sojourn at the seminary. In sacrificing to his attraction for the foreign missions his aspirations to the monastic state, he had lost nothing of the spirit of his primitive vocation; and his great joy on entering the Seminary of the Rue du Bac had been to find in this holy community what was equivalent to the religious life.

"There is one thing here," he writes to a former fellow-student at Issy, "that pleases me greatly: holy poverty is practised. The seminary receives no pension for the student, but alms only. He is lodged, fed, supported by the seminary. All that he possesses, all that he finds in his cell—books, furniture, clothing—all are furnished him by the house or by his friends. What pleasure this gives me, in thus bringing me nearer the monastic life, and establishing among us all a community of goods! What happiness to be able to say, I eat the bread of charity!"

We shall soon see to what perfection Just brought the love and the practice of poverty. Now, however, we are still taking a glance at the first weeks of his sojourn here. His virtues have already won the esteem of his fellow-students; but Just regards himself as an intruder into the society of saints, and his letters are full of the admiration excited in him at sight of all he sees around him. "Up to the present time," he writes to a priest of the diocese of Dijon, "I am more and more confirmed in the belief that the good God calls me to His service in the foreign missions; the thought grows stronger day by day....Time passes for me with extreme rapidity, and with no more pre-occupation of mind than if I were never to leave my native land. Moreover, let me assure you that the prospect of separation does not in the least cast a gloom over the inmates of this house. On the contrary, there is perhaps no other community where frank gayety reigns as openly as it does here, the good God already recompensing the first sacrifices and the desire for greater ones by perfect tranquillity of soul.

And the nearer the time of trial approaches, the more does
Divine Providence take possession of these hearts, long
since given it, and fill them with a simplicity, an infantine
sweetness, truly astonishing, could they witness it, to all
those whom God has not favored with the grace of comprehending the happiness of such a state.

"Our Lord diffuses also among these future apostles a
charity with which it were an impossibility not to be struck,
even at first sight. Here all are brothers, forming but one
body ; and we may say in truth that directors and aspirants
have but one heart, one soul, their thoughts, their desires,
being one. That ardent love which the Apostle St. John
so recommends to his disciples unites all the members of
this community. . . . Here there is need of greater virtues
than elsewhere; of humility, abnegation, devotedness; and
here too are they found, in so high a degree that as for
me, a poor beginner, I can scarcely comprehend them."

There was even a short period about this time when
the spectacle of these sublime virtues, carried to such perfection, proved to him a trial, a sort of momentary temptation, which he afterwards revealed to his mother in confidence. In contemplating before God the sanctity of those
with whom he was going to ally his life, in measuring
the merits of these directors, several of whom had confessed the Faith under torture, he had been seized with
fear. Was it a passing weakness of nature at the prospect of
the sacrifices in store for him? Or was it the mere out-
come of a timid, shrinking disposition, habitually mistrusting its fitness for any undertaking? Perhaps it was both.
But this hesitation vanished, and Just understood that God
had allowed him to realize, for a moment, his own weakness,
only to afford him the occasion for an act of renewed generosity and confidence. Summoning then all his energy,
he fearlessly faces the heights which have been shown him,

and beginning their ascent, remembers no longer his infirmity, except to exact more of that will which he had given to God, and which for an instant had wavered.

The recollections of his former fellow-students, to-day missionaries in various lands, indicate to us the heroic programme which he henceforth traced out for himself, ever remaining inviolably faithful to it. According to it, the aspirant should make all his actions a preparation for the apostolic life. The apostle is poor: he immediately embraced the most stringent poverty. Wishing to wear nothing but what came under the head of alms, he divided among his brethren all the linen and other articles of apparel which he had brought to the seminary, and henceforth received from the charity of his superior everything that he wore. He had but one cassock, which he wore until it was falling to pieces, after being patched times innumerable; his underclothing was so threadbare and torn that a beggar would not have wanted it, yet he continued to wear it. Among a lot of suitable hats from which each aspirant makes a choice is a shabby one of coarse felt; this Just selects, and no other will he have until his departure, so that Father de Breteniéres' hat becomes proverbial in the house.

Perceiving one day that his neck-tie is so worn as to be really unfit for use, he thinks of asking for another; but in the meantime, accidentally finding one in the sweepings of the seminary corridor, he appropriates it, saying as he does so, "This is better than mine."

The apostle is ever on the cross: Just resolved to inure himself to suffering. Did he practise those macerations of the body in vogue among the religious orders? They who knew him best have been unable to say; but his preferences were evidently for the mortifications most calculated to prepare him for the rough life of the missionary. During his first year at the seminary he accustomed himself to sleeping in his clothing.   In winter he put the straw mattress on top to make his bed harder; in summer he slept on the floor.   Did he come in bathed in perspiration or drenched with rain, he never changed his clothing.   And with him this was no affectation of austerity: he was endeavoring to harden himself to the inclemencies of the weather, of which the missionary should take no account.   The virile education he had received rendered him capable of supporting such hardships.   Sometimes, however, he went too far.   In the vacation of 1862, after a geological excursion of two days in a pouring rain, sleeping two nights in his soaking garments, he was taken with inflammation on the chest, which left behind an obstinate cough.   His health was seriously compromised for a time.   His mother noticed that the freshness of youth had disappeared from his altered countenance and given place to a deadly pallor; but neither she nor any other member of his family knew until some time afterwards, how narrow had been his escape from a dread malady!   As to the cough, he concealed it the best he could, declining their visits for three weeks to prevent them seeing to what a pitiable state it had reduced him.   Yet he would not suffer this prolonged indisposition to interrupt any of his ordinary occupations.   "For three months," he writes to his former preceptor, "I have been suffering from a cough, which does not appear as if it were going to leave me very soon.   It fatigues and wears me, but this is of small account."

In proportion as he advances towards the priesthood his love of suffering increases.   At Meudon he selects for his cell a little place immediately under the roof, where the heat is so insupportable that at night he is obliged to rise in order to seek a little air through a narrow opening in the roof, which serves as a window.

He learns also to conquer sleep.   Profiting by the general

permission, he does not retire until ten o'clock; and at Meudon, where the rule is less rigorous, his accumulated occupations often keep him out of bed until eleven o'clock, yet he is always up at four in the morning, in the vacations frequently anticipating the time for rising by three quarters of an hour.

The apostle is obedient. Regretting that he was not under religious obedience, Just hastened to make a vow of obedience to his superior and director, M. Albrand, submitting to him everything that he undertook—his studies, his works of zeal and of charity, his mortifications, visits, correspondence. From the second year of his sojourn here, he is a man truly dead to self, inured to sacrifice.

The apostle is a butt for contempt. Just has a proud soul, and shudders at the thought of humiliation, as letters written by him to his friends at the seminary bear ample testimony. But he has resolved never to yield to the repugnances of nature. Hence he makes small account of seeking the most humble employments and performing the most menial services. He will not consider himself a missionary until, like the saints, he shall have courted opprobrium and raillery. One day, whilst walking out with the whole community, in the market quarters of Paris, he adds to the oddness of his usual appearance in the shabby garb he habitually wore by a singular attitude, thus attracting the ridicule and jeers of passers-by, in which humiliation he rejoices.

Worldly souls cannot conceive of mortification as separable from sadness; in their eyes an austere life must needs be gloomy and desolate. But oh ! what a mistake, for cheerfulness is characteristic of all who make war upon self.

Just was no exception to this rule. After one year at the Seminary of the Rue du Bac, during which time he had already advanced with rapid step along the rough road on which he had entered, he writes thus to his old preceptor: "I feel here as I never did at Issy; I am really so very happy that I cannot but think I am dreaming, all this cannot be a reality." About this same time, and as if to show that the joy of the saints does not place them above the weaknesses of nature, he confesses frankly to his brother that there are moments when his interior anguish is great at thoughts of leaving his family and friends forever. "I cannot think without shuddering," he says, "of the moment when I must bid a final adieu to my father, mother, relatives, country. Oh ! how incapable I should be of this immolation if left to myself ! Without God's grace it were impossible. But I have confidence: God will aid me. Is this not a case in which we must repeat the words of St. Ambrose, ' The saints were not of a different race from ourselves; they were only more faithful:' *Naturæ non præstantioris, sed observantioris?*"

The end of this first year was marked for Just by a painful trial. Having entered the Rue du Bac with the tonsure, he expected to receive Minor Orders at the Trinity ordinations, as is customary at St. Sulpice; being ignorant of the fact that the rule of the Seminary of Foreign Missions requires the aspirant to have passed a whole year in the house, ere receiving any of the orders. The names were called and his was not among them. This omission, had it not been in consequence of the rule above mentioned, might signify that his superiors did not deem him qualified for apostolic work. He imparted in confidence to his brother the anguish of his soul at this.

"I have been for two days bowed down," he says, "beneath the weight of this measure, which seems to me inexplicable; for on sounding my heart I cannot doubt my vocation. However, before speaking to my director and confiding to him my sorrow, I will offer to God the entire sac-

rifice of my aspirations, if needs be, and submit myself to
His will.   I am in a state of constant agitation; it seems to
me impossible for me not to become a missionary.   My
nights are sleepless; when I feel myself growing too despond-
ent and grieved, I softly hum some hymn or canticle in
honor of the Blessed Virgin, to whom I have committed
my interests.   This soothes me and restores my courage.   I
then feel better disposed to comply with all that the good
God desires of me."   Adds his brother: "It was not until
after reducing his poor heart, if not to a state of indiffer-
ence, at least to complete resignation, that he made known
his trouble to M. Albrand.   The latter immediately re-
assured him, by explaining the cause that delayed his ordination to the Christmas ember days."

The following year, when with joyful soul he was preparing for the holy engagements of the sub-deaconate, a
trial of another nature menaced his happiness.   Misled by
some gossip he had heard, one knows not where, a priest of
the diocese of Dijon, imagining that Just's virtue was not
up to the high standard the Church requires of her clerics
ere engaging in the more advanced grades of Holy Orders,
wrote him a severe letter, charging him with rashness in
persisting to continue in a course of life to which he had
not been called by God, but impelled thereon by spite alone.
This was a warning to him, it said, which he would do well
to consider even as the voice of God, urging him to repent
and stop on the brink of the precipice.   Troubled at first
by this language, Just once more questioned his heart.
"Thou knowest, my God," said he, "whether my intentions
are pure, and whether I have ever loved anything but Thee."
Praying much, he recovered his peace of soul, and fearlessly broke through the last barrier that could have turned his steps from the priesthood.

When a soul is entirely given to God, it cannot rest satisfied without striving to make others imitate its example, and thus share its happiness. Charity impels it thereto, almost beyond the power of resistance; and inexperience sometimes allows it to take steps that discretion condemns —a fault, however, very excusable in one who has not had sufficient acquaintance with souls so as to be initiated into their weaknesses, and who has not learned how to discern the diverse ways of Providence. Just's correspondence furnishes us an example of this zeal, perhaps mistaken, which time would not fail to correct and mature. Yet even here, how could one refrain from admiring the ardor of that language in which love for Jesus Christ inspired him?

An ecclesiastic whom Just knew in the world had made an attempt at the religious life, but without persevering therein. Devoting himself afterwards to teaching, he had always recoiled from the responsibilities of the priesthood, and remained in Minor Orders. Pious, however, and nourishing in the depths of his heart a vague regret for his primitive vocation, he envied our young aspirant's fervor without bringing himself to imitate it. To have remained within the bounds of prudence, Just should have contented himself with exhorting him to become a priest and thus serve the Church in the holy ministry, for there was nothing about his friend indicating the least attraction or qualification for the foreign apostolate. But with Just to be a priest was to be a missionary; he could not conceive otherwise of the priesthood. "When I think that in three or four years," said he one day to the writer of these lines, as we were leaving a church in Paris, "you will doubtless be vicar at St. Roche's, or something analogous to it, it seems to me so strange; I really cannot comprehend it." After eighteen months' sojourn at the Seminary of the Missions, when he felt more attracted by grace than ever to the complete immolation of self, this disposition to regard the priest as ever identical with the missionary but increased in his soul. He now persuaded himself that the ecclesiastic of whom we speak stifled within his heart, either through weakness or thoughtlessness, a vocation similar to his own, and he entered into a correspondence with him which reveals the ardor of Just's sentiments. We borrow from one of the most important of these letters a quotation, for the length of which no one will reproach us, for in the history of the true servants of God their own words are always best. Just writes as follows:

"I find a striking contradiction in your letter. You say to me in one place: 'Am I then of the world? Do I esteem anything more than heaven, than the saving of a soul?' And elsewhere you say, 'I am now nearly forty years old, a man who has fixed habits of rising, retiring, eating, drinking, etc. Ah! truly my whole being shudders at the thought you propose!. . . . I cannot resolve to follow you even to the Rue du Bac.'

"How does this appear to you? Can these two assertions be true of the same person? I can scarcely believe it.

"If it be true that you are of the number of those men enslaved by miserable little habits, of those who shudder at the thought of becoming humble and obedient, appalled at the idea of entering a community—if unhappily you are of that number, I tell you that you are wofully mistaken in believing yourself not of the world; for he is of the world who relies upon anything except our divine Saviour. You are mistaken in believing that you esteem nothing more than heaven; for he who prizes heaven as he should places under foot all those little comforts of which you speak; he heeds God's voice when it calls him, and does not say as you do, 'I feel within me something urging me to go with you to China or to Cochin China, and yet I cannot resolve to ac-

company you even to the Rue du Bac.' I also tell you that
you deceive yourself most wofully if you believe that you
value nothing more than the price of a soul. Oh! he who
realizes the value of a soul, and esteems nothing so much
as to work for its salvation, takes slight account of anything
this requires of him. He would laugh in astonishment if
some one should say to him, ' But consider that you have
your regular habits of eating, drinking, rising, retiring,
and all these you must give up! ' Would he ever imagine
for an instant that this involved any sacrifice? Oh! can
he who realizes the value of a soul think of anything else?
If there is anything in the world that can impel one to ex-
ceed all bounds, is it not love for souls? for love for souls is
inseparable from the folly of the holy love for Jesus Christ.
And he who is filled with it becomes mad; nothing arrests
his course, no sacrifice deters him, or rather I should say,
he seeks to make sacrifices, and complains of not finding
them. Nor does he find them. He believed it a sacrifice
to leave his family, and it was not—it was a holocaust of
joy. He believed it a sacrifice to quit those places to
which he was attached; friends with whom he seemed one,
so that living without them appeared to him impossible;
to break with hopes that smile on others: sacrifices they
were that began for him a Paradise on earth. Love for
souls possesses all his thoughts; he traverses seas never
dreaming of the perils which he courts; he will thrill with
joy if God lead him to places where everything threatens
his life, unable to restrain his songs of exultation at beholding himself exposed to persecution, threatened with
the sword, even on the point of dying from famine, fatigue,
sorrow, anguish; and yet with all this he believes that he
has suffered little, because he still sees souls deaf to grace.
He conjures Our Lord to make him suffer more; this love
of suffering is with him a consuming thirst which nothing

appeases, for he is mad with the enviable madness of love
for God.   Behold the picture of one who prizes a soul at
its real value—the true servant of God, whom Our Lord
will not deny at the last day.   I pity them who through
contempt or neglect of graces are not as he whom I have
just described, for their last hour will be terrible.   And
you—on which side do you range yourself, you whom
only miserable little habits of comfort arrest, whom only
the thought of submitting yourself to the sweet yoke of
obedience can render deaf to the appeals of a poor soul
that a little courage on your part might have saved from
hell!   I think this a very serious matter; I do not know
whether you agree with me.

" You promised to ask for me the signal grace of martyrdom, but on condition that I would ask the same for you.
What! can you believe that God would grant such a favor,
such a recompense inestimable, to one who will not sacrifice
to His glory even a few moments of repose, a few creature
comforts, whilst often refusing it to hundreds of missionaries, who consecrate themselves unreservedly to Him?   And
let me here remark that we must not deem God unjust in refusing them this grace, for although He denies them the signal favor of shedding their blood for Him, thus gaining an
immortal crown, He reserves for them another crown not
less glorious—the martyrdom of thirty years of mission life;
for this, aye, even much less, equals the martyrdom of
blood.   But God surely will not lavish the grace of martyrdom on one who will make no sacrifices in advance.   Do
you not know that martyrdom is the heroic act of love?
How, then, could he be a martyr who does not love?   And
it is not loving God to love anything except Him, or apart
from Him.   Pardon me for saying it, but it seems to me that
if I were in your place I should blush in asking martyrdom
so long as I did not blush in refusing God the most trifling

sacrifice.   Pardon me for saying all this, dear friend, but I must tell you what I think.   Moreover, I should blush at approaching the Holy Table, if hearing within me a voice urging me to give myself entirely to God, I made reply, Yes, my Jesus, Thou hast given Thyself to me unreservedly, unconditionally, Thou hast descended into the vile depths of my heart, Thou hast submitted Thyself to me, begging in return only that I give myself to Thee as unreservedly. Thou dost urge me to this in the gentlest, sweetest manner, promising me Thy love in recompense.   Thou speakest to me as a friend to a friend, a brother to a brother, showing me all that Thy love has inspired Thee to do and to suffer for me.   Yet I cannot respond to Thy invitation, some things hold me back and come between us—my comforts, my conveniences; I am more attached to them than to Thee!

" Behold, dear friend, a true picture of your conduct; I do not think I have exaggerated it.   No doubt, you deem me under an illusion on this point, but I fear this is rather your case than mine.   You asked me to speak frankly, and I have tried my best to do so, moved thereto solely by the desire of God's greater glory and your own soul's good.

" What do you think of my words?   With what reflections do they inspire you?   May the good God sustain you herein and His mercy overshadow you!

" Instead of looking at the difficulties in your path, cast yourself at God's feet, humble yourself before Him, and acknowledge that heretofore you have been slothful and lukewarm in His service.

." Ask His pardon for your weakness, and then recovering confidence, raise your courage, for God Himself will come to your assistance.   Pray, pray much and earnestly, for it is in prayer you will find the needed strength.   I think of you all the time, I can almost say, without exaggeration, day and night. I pray for you myself all I can, and I feel confident that God will arouse you from your torpor. But you must do something towards it yourself. God wishes you all for Himself; give yourself to Him then without reserve, and He, in turn, will not fail to reward you, even on earth, for the missionary's temporal recompense always outweighs any sacrifice he could make: *Qui habet aures audiendi, audiat! Beatus qui intelligit!*

" You wished a long letter, dear friend, and I think you have reason to be satisfied on this point. God grant it may be thus in some other respects. There are still some things that I should like to say to you, but our good Mother knows how to inspire you with them much better than I could ever bring them before you.

" I must now finish my letter, not, however, without saying that I have written under no external influence, but solely from my own heart; so that whatever there may be reprehensible in my words must be attributed to me alone. Behold now at your feet, your poor, proud, despicable friend, always the same, or, rather, truly more despicable than ever. I really wonder how, considering my own spiritual poverty, I have been able to speak to you as I have done. The sole desire of procuring your happiness has urged me thereto. But be under no illusions regarding me. If you need prayers, I have still greater need of them, and the good God must be merciful indeed to suffer my presence in this house. There is no one here who has probably offended Him so much as myself ; hence I should ever do penance and, above all, implore pardon unceasingly. Pray much for me, then, in view of my spiritual destitution and my nothingness; for the future missionary's charity and affection should, like his divine Master's, embrace the whole world, and you know how lacking I am in these virtues. You may rest assured of my prayers for you: there is nothing I would not do to increase your happiness. Ever yours in Jesus and Mary."

This letter is dated **July 12, 1862.** The writer was but twenty-four years old, and he had had no experience of the world; he had been in the Seminary of the Missions scarce more than a year and had not yet received Minor Orders. These circumstances, whilst sufficing to excuse whatever may appear intemperate in his zeal, likewise constrain us to admire the work of grace which, in so short a time, had so exalted this faithful soul that it was unable to comprehend aught incompatible with perfect renunciation, perfect love.

If such was Just's zeal in endeavoring to draw his friends to the apostolic vocation, one can well imagine what it must have been in initiating therein, and encouraging those whom this vocation placed near him in the seminary. Of this all his fellow-students, now missionaries, have borne witness in the letters which they wrote to his parents on hearing of his martyrdom. We borrow some extracts from one of these letters, which serves as a specimen of all the rest. The writer says:

"That I have persevered in my vocation is, under God, due to him. I entered the Seminary of the Missions in September, 1863, and on the day of my arrival I was taken to Meudon. This first day, spent in visits to the Rev. directors and to my new brethren, passed without weariness. But next morning, finding myself alone, I directed my steps towards the woods, plunged in sad thoughts at having left my friends, my family, and, above all, my mother who had been paralyzed for the last six years. Suddenly I was joined by your holy son, who with a smiling countenance kindly greeted me. Questioning me, he lent a gracious ear to all the outpourings of my heart; and his gentle words restored peace to my soul. . . . But later on I was again a prey to trouble, and beset by temptations—both ever increasing. At last, yielding to

weariness and distress, I several times thought of quitting
the seminary, yet did not dare to carry out the resolution.
I opened my heart a little to Father B.; after which,
through him and Father D., I was placed in close relations
with your son. Whenever the memory of my country, my
family, or of others whom I loved, tormented me, or the
temptations of the demon threatened to abase me, I went
to him; and no matter what the hour, he was always ready
to receive me, always affable, full of suavity, goodness,
and amiable gayety. Making me sit down, he would take
a seat beside me on his little bed. 'Silly child,' he would
say, 'so you wish to go, you wish to leave the good God!'
And then he would speak to me of the missions, of the
good God, of the happiness of serving Him, of heaven,
etc., so gently and soothingly that I would return entirely consoled and encouraged. His charity even made him
abase himself before me to relieve my confusion, which he
saw was great on account of my sins and temptations. He
moreover did this so well by his words, representing himself such a sinner, that I was almost shaken in the idea I
had of his sanctity, and was tempted to believe that he had
sinned in his youth. One evening after Just's departure,
when I was out walking with Mgr. Charbonnier, Vicar
Apostolic of Eastern Cochin China, he spoke to us of the
innocence of Just's early years. I was struck with his
words, and could not forbear exclaiming, 'The deceiver!
Why did he try to make me believe that he was such a
sinner!'

"However, he had not succeeded in persuading me of
this; for one day, just before the departure of some of our
brethren for the missions, as I held him by the hand whilst
he spoke to another candidate and myself of God, his words
were so penetrating, his hand so burning that I could not
help thinking, It is love for God that thus inflames him.

" Even after leaving us, his charity did not permit him to forget me. Besides praying much for me, he wrote to me, and his letters, souvenirs of friendship, came from the far East to the depths of Anjou, whither sickness had forced me to return. I have two letters from him in which I have the happiness of seeing myself addressed as ' dear little Louis,' ' my very dear little Louis.' One is dated from Notre Dame du Soleil (Mantchooria), April 19, 1865: the other from Séoul (Corea), August 10, of the same year. In both of these he shows his deep charity in the sorrow which he expresses on hearing that I have been obliged to return home on account of ill health. He urges me to profit by this trial, and assures me that I am not forgotten in his prayers. After thus encouraging me, he adds these humble words : ' And do you likewise pray much and fervently for the poor, miserable creature now writing to you—for him whose heart is so cold, and who does so little to make Our Lord forget his ingratitude.' A passage in the second letter evinces at the same time both his charitable friendship and his love of mortification. ' Take good care of yourself,' he writes, ' for health is very necessary to the missionary. Mortifications throng in upon him from every side, without his having to seek them. This is why the missionary's life is so abundant in good to his own soul. Farewell. Write to me every year, and may Our Lord reign in our hearts.' "

Love for souls knows no barriers. Although such a friend to solitude in the seminary, Just eagerly seized upon the occasions which offered to apply himself to those exterior works that obedience and the usages of the house permitted him to undertake. The two principal were visiting the old men in the house of the Little Sisters of the Poor, in the Rue St. Jacques, and *the apostolate of the quarries.*

It was really a great happiness for him to pass some hours with the poor old men, listening to their histories, consoling and serving them. His sympathy induced them to open their hearts to him, and he made use of this confidence to lead them to God. Loving and revering in them the poverty of Jesus Christ, he never showed the least weariness of their conversation. "Oh! the poor! the dear poor!" he exclaimed one day, on leaving the house with one of his brethren; "are they not more agreeable to God than all these people passing by with their luxury and vanity?"

The work of the quarries interested and occupied him even more than the above. It had been begun some time before his entrance into the Seminary of the Missions. The house of the community at Meudon is but a short distance from the stone-quarries furnishing the building materials for Paris and its environs. The quarrymen spend nearly all their lives here in the hardest kind of labor, forming a distinct class of the population on the outskirts of the city. The gross ignorance in which they live tends to make them forget God, and all sorts of vices are the consequence. The directors of the seminary, seeing herein for their candidates a beautiful opportunity of exercising themselves in the apostolic ministry, permitted the most fervent and edifying of them to devote to this work the leisure of their vacations and holy-days. Just, initiated therein by the two of his brethren to whom he was most attached, soon became, in turn, their model, by reason of his zeal and practical charity. Beginning with some friendly words to the laborers, some technical questions about the work, these young men, thus gaining their confidence by degrees, expressed an interest in them, which took a substantial shape. Was one of the quarrymen sick, had he an aged, infirm father, or was there among them an orphan needing a home, the aspi-

rants would immediately proffer help, volunteering to aid
from their own poverty a poverty more stringent and less
voluntary.   Just's letters to his parents, about this time,
are full of appeals, now unobtrusive, now pressing, for the
means of fulfilling many such promises.   Once in possession of the confidence of these good people, the young
aspirants to the priesthood commenced to instruct them,
speaking to them of God, and striving to raise towards
heaven their souls bowed down to earth, all unconscious of
their dignity.   Just was really to be remarked for the fervor
of his exhortations.   Yet always endeavoring to place himself beneath others, he cheerfully gave his companions the
precedence on all occasions, even stopping short in his instructions whenever they or the quarrymen had anything
which they wished to say.   This humility thus practised
before man, had its source in that greater humility causing
him to abase himself before God.

Before approaching the laborers, he would say to one of
his brethren, "Let us humble ourselves in the presence of
God; and let us acknowledge that without His grace we
would be more ignorant and sinful than these poor creatures.   And, moreover, who knows but that even now they
stand higher in God's eyes than we who abuse so many
graces?"

A letter he wrote to his parents shows us his manner of
proceeding in the apostolate of the quarries.   He says, "I
first persuade myself—and it is easily done—that these
people may be better than myself.   I must have this feeling towards them not only as regards their virtue, but
their birth, which it is necessary to leave out of sight.
They are men like ourselves, children of God like ourselves,
and we should speak and deal with them as our fellow-
creatures, standing on a level with ourselves....I seek to
gain a soul, and I see it dwelling in a body, so fatigued by

work as to be nearly exhausted. Casting aside my hat, my book, I take off my cassock, and rolling up my sleeves, seizes the pick-axe, the handspike, the crow-bar, and make an effort to aid him materially; very often I thus instruct him regarding his work, by raising the stone and turning it with more facility than he does. And when he is persuaded that, although wearing a cassock, I am a man like himself, little by little I raise his thoughts to spiritual things, bringing to him, by speaking of God and His law, those lights which he lacked hereupon; very often truth reveals itself to him, and he is converted.... Were I at Bretenières, I would do the same, commencing always by convincing myself that I was no better than those whom I sought to aid; nay, that they were perhaps better than I: then I would act in a frank, straightforward manner, speaking with simplicity, and showing my interest in these people by the charity with which I desired their welfare." Again he recurs to this subject. "In dealings with the poor and the peasantry of Bretenières," he writes, "cast aside all vanity, all idea of superiority; work with them, serve them, show them how to improve upon what they do, and then, when you speak to them of the good God they will believe you."

Certainly these are counsels which few Christians seem capable of understanding, for they express nothing less than the highest evangelical perfection; and to follow them one must be already dead to self. That they appear little applicable must be attributed to the feeble virtue of those who call themselves disciples of Jesus Christ. Christian morals alone, if seriously prized and practised to the letter, would resolve what men style the social problem.

Mme. de Bretenières furnishes us with a little anecdote which we here relate in termination of our account of the apostolate of the quarries.

On one of the coldest winter days Just had gone to the quarries with Father D. Missing from the audience an old man hitherto very punctual in attendance, and inquiring the cause of his absence, they learned that he was ill of fever, and lying sheltered in one of the cavities of the rocks. At once the future apostles began a search for him—an undertaking which the darkness of the night rendered very difficult. Having at last reached an abandoned quarry, they heard some one calling out and threatening them violently. It was the poor old man, who supposing them robbers come to make an attempt on his pocket and his life, sought thus to frighten them off. After considerable difficulty in making themselves known to him, they approached; and perceiving that he would certainly perish from cold if left there, they took him upon their shoulders, and in spite of the difficulties of the road, increased by the darkness of night, they carried him thus to the hospital at Sèvres. But their task was not finished; there was not one vacant bed at the hospital. Going from door to door with the sick man, begging shelter for him, they at last found an inn-keeper who received him, and relying upon their honesty, contented himself for the present with the sum of ten cents (all the money they had about them), promising them to wait for the remainder and take care of the sick man until there was a vacant bed at the hospital. It was after eleven o'clock at night when the two aspirants re-entered the seminary.

We have re-united in one picture certain characteristic traits of the virtues which shone in our candidate. Virtue is, in fact, a holy habit, acquired by repeated acts, each one of which appears little in itself, and not worthy of narration: it is in their entirety we must present them if we wish to make apparent the result of daily efforts herein. We are now going to note in chronological order the prin-

cipal events marking Just's three years' sojourn at the Seminary of the Missions. Borrowing the details, as we do, from
his letters, from the recollections of his parents, of his brother, of his fellow-students, we shall be obliged to return,
more than once, to subjects which we have already touched
upon. The reader will pardon us these inevitable repetitions in the story of an existence so barren of incidents as
that of a seminarian, especially as he will find throughout
what he seeks in this history—edification.

The first year was for Just the epoch of what he called
his *second conversion*, the first having taken place at Issy,
according to his own statement. This expression, familiar
to the saints, astonishes the worldly, and yet it is strictly
exact. To be converted is to change one's course. One is
converted when he passes from sin to grace; this conversion
the holy young man did not need. But one is also converted when he passes from ordinary piety to that higher
form of understanding the soul's communications with God.
His entrance at Issy had signalized for Just a first change
of this sort; the early part of his sojourn at the Rue du
Bac accomplished in him a second change, deeper than
the first. He saw more clearly the end he was to pursue
and the best means of doing so; even his mistakes of inexperience show traces of that inconquerable resolution impelling him towards perfection. Thus, realizing that humility must be the foundation of the spiritual edifice, " he
began," writes a missionary who was one of his fellow-
students, " by so extraordinary a sentiment of his own
nothingness, that he really believed himself unworthy to
be found in the midst of his brethren. As he told me himself, he dared not raise his eyes to them. The result of
such interior struggles was a spell of sickness; and those who
had the care of him remarked truly that the cause lay
rather in the moral than in the physical nature. A word

from his director restored his peace of soul, and guided him in the way of humility."

So again, wishing to prepare both himself and his parents for the final separation, he began by attempting to break off nearly all communication with them. But soon understanding that such a course was wholly incompatible with his duty towards a father and a mother who had, in no wise, resisted God's will in his regard, he resumed his usual affectionate relations with them, without relaxing any of his regularity, or encroaching upon his works and studies, frequently borrowing from his nights the time given his parents.

Thus passed his first year at the seminary. When after the vacation of 1862, spent entirely at Mendon, Just again took up his studies and accustomed exercises, a great change had been wrought in him. His humility was profound, and his energy had grown proportionately. There was a firmness, an indescribably resolute manner denoting a vocation sure of itself. Compared to the backward, timid seminarian who but one short year ago had crossed the threshold of the missionaries' house, one could say that he was already another man. How rare are they who in twelve months make such progress in the paths of spirituality! Truly, they understand what is understood by few, and what Father Olivaint, another valiant Christian, formulates in these words: "It takes less of time than of will to make a saint."

The Christmas ordinations saw Just advanced to Minor Orders. For this he prepared himself with extraordinary fervor, beholding at only a few months' distance from this preliminary initiation his consecration to the sub-deaconate.

It was during this second year that his brother's vocation began to be more clearly marked out. It appears as if Just must have had a presentiment of this from about the time of the vacations of 1862; for writing now to Christian regarding a friend of the latter who had decided to quit the world, he says: " So B. leaves you alone in the world, choosing for himself the better part. I think that notwithstanding the pain you must feel at thought of the separation from him, you cannot but congratulate him on having heard and heeded the voice of God calling him to a life infinitely more sweet and full of charms than that which he leaves....Esteem him happy then; and if ever you hear, like him, God's blessed voice inviting you to the same favors, ah! do not close your ears to it; for the cup presented to your lips contains a most delicious beverage, although the first taste may have the bitterness of gall.... If God's designs upon you are not the same as those which He has upon your friend, humble yourself before Him, and with great fear embrace this life in the world; in a word, whilst living in an empoisoned atmosphere, let your conduct be guided not by the principles of worldlings, but by those of the religious, although, unlike these latter, you have not the happiness of being the child of God's predilection."

Six months later he takes another step in this matter, still acting with that discretion which fears to anticipate God's workings. " In all my instructions regarding your studies and labors," he writes to Christian, " do not lose sight of a most important point, which perhaps you do not understand. I am like a bell, having but one tone, and I repeat to you over and over, 'All is vanity except to love God.' Oh! what happiness for me, if before leaving you I could, with God's grace, make you foresee the dawn of a day as yet unknown to you. This do I earnestly desire for you, a thousand times more than the most brilliant career. Implore God from the depths of your heart, every time you receive Holy Communion, that He will make you understand what it is to live for Him."

A few days later he writes again: "You seem to me like that soul mentioned in the *Imitation*, ever seeking the place destined for it by divine Providence, yet all unconscious of such search, and unable to account to itself for what it does. You have not yet found the point of union; with God's help, *you must find it within yourself.* Keep your soul in peace, your quest will not be vain; but to expedite the coming of the happy day which assures you the object of your research, bear ever in mind that nothing out of God will satisfy you, no matter how strong your convictions be to the contrary."

It was towards the commencement of this second year that Just was admitted to the apostolate of the quarries. He announces this good news to one of his old friends, already a missionary in Siam, with whom during the preceding year his relations had been those of friendly intimacy, and to whom he frequently wrote, desiring to excite himself to fervor by continued communication with so holy a soul. Humility, self-contempt, the ardor of good desires form the pith of this correspondence, and one perceives in each successive letter increasing energy of will in the pursuit of perfection. "Every time you speak to me of loving Jesus," Just writes, "I feel my heart stirred, my desire to love Him grow stronger; but alas! how fruitless these desires! always the same cowardice, the same ingratitude!....I realize that there is but one thing I must ask for both you and myself—love. Oh! *quis dabit mihi pennas sicut columbæ, et volabo?*....Father, it will not be more than a year before I am a priest. Can it be possible that Jesus will raise me so high—I who am truly vile and contemptible? I can scarce pray, for I am appalled at the thought, and already tremble at it."

We here note another advance in spirituality. One year previously, his heart was wrung in anticipation of the great sacrifice, the final separation. This troubles him no longer; it is the priesthood and fear of his unworthiness for this august office that now absorb his mind and heart—a fear which, inspired and combated by love, will only continue to increase in his soul. Some weeks before the last ordination, which was to take place very near the time for his departure, the writer of these lines said to him, "Just, which occupies your thoughts the most now, the ordination or the farewells?"—"What nonsense!" he answered pleasantly, "I think of the priesthood only; the other never troubles me. My friend, my dear friend, can you realize, that I, I am going to say Mass?" And at this his face was radiant with joy.

In another letter to the same missionary we find the expression of his increasing love for poverty. "The next time you write to me," he says, "I would like you to tell me, if you deem it not inadvisable, what is your opinion of poverty for the missionary. For my part, I never had any other idea than that of one day embracing a life not only of affective but of effective poverty. If there had been a religious order *exclusively devoted to the Missions,* and requiring of its members a vow of poverty, I think that would have been my choice. The ardor of my desire for poverty increases daily. It seems to me that all I read, all I see or hear, whispers to me, 'You should be stripped of everything, in the strictest sense of the term; keep only what is absolutely necessary for your present wants, and get rid of everything else.' I am often reasoned with to prove that affective poverty suffices; yet, in the depths of my heart I feel something which urges me to go farther, and everything that I hear to the contrary has no effect upon me. Probably I am talking nonsense in thus expressing my opinion of what I do not understand; and no doubt the missions will teach me to practise a more perfect poverty

than any I now desire or comprehend.   Perhaps I am blind
and proud."

In fact, Just acknowledged a little later on that effective
poverty is found in the highest degree in the missionary's
ordinary life, as we learn from Mme. de Bretenières' notes of
conversations with him, during his last year at the seminary.
He says: "The missionary is poorer than any religious;
whilst the Carthusian knows that to-morrow he will receive
his allowance of food as he did to-day, the missionary eating his frugal meal is not sure of the next.   And indeed he
does not always get it.   He is even ignorant of the extent
of the privations that threaten him; but withal he must
needs keep up his courage, and preserve his equanimity of
mind."

With the growing love for poverty, that for recollection
became more and more active in his soul.   As is ever the
case, in revealing anything of God's graces he always joined
thereto an imputation of his own weakness; but such is
the language of the saints, their humility knows no other.
"I feel most sensibly, and with continuously increasing
force," he says, "that Our Lord demands of me uninter-
rupted recollection, no matter what my occupations.
This thought is ever before my mind. (What is this if it
be not true recollection?)   Yet it does not suffice for this
that in the depths of my heart I remain strongly united
to Our L.   especially when engaged in something which
interests me and claims a little of my attention."   A letter which he writes from Corea to one of his brethren, a
missionary in Birmah, shows us that the humble candidate
had in reality been faithful to this attraction.   We read
therein the following passage: "Do you still remember
the good-will God bestowed upon us at the seminary, and the
attraction with which he inspired us for recollection and
the drawing nearer to Himself?   As for me, when I re-

call that blessed time, I feel all inflamed with holy desires."

Spring at last arrives and brings to Just the happy news of his call to the sub-deaconate. His soul literally overflows with joy. "For years," he writes, "have I desired the coming of this day; or, to speak more truly, I have never desired anything else."

It is on the 30th of May, 1863, that he takes the decisive step. His parents are in Paris; so jealous is he to preserve recollection that he writes few letters to outsiders at this time; hence we find scarce any souvenirs of those sentiments of fervor which, according to his mother, shone forth brilliantly in him, both at the approach and the end of his consecration. But the progress of his virtue became visible to all, and revealed something of the secret love then exchanged between his soul and God.

The scholastic year is finished, and the vacations again bring the community to Meudon. Just is more engaged than ever in his works of zeal; he has also, unknown to himself, acquired an ascendancy over his brethren, and he must give much of his time to them; finally, he is more devoted than ever to prayer. In consequence of all this, his correspondence with his parents suffers, his letters to them becoming less frequent. In each one, however, he tenderly proffers his excuses. His language too has lost that affected stiffness by which he formerly sought to preserve himself from weakness. His brother's vocation is now matured. Under the firm, gentle direction of Mgr. de Segur, to whom he confided the care of his soul, Christian has seen his doubts disappear. He has resolved to enter the seminary at Issy, at the end of vacation. The elder brother encourages and guides him in this resolution, by counsels stamped with experience in God's ways. Whilst father and son make together a geological excursion, Just accompanies them with his interest and advice, ever careful not to lose sight of their souls. To his father he sends words of tender deference, yet full of supernatural vigor; and speaking as if the paternal heart possessed all that firmness which he desired for it, he respectfully tenders encouragement and exhortation under the cover of thanks. Knowing that the hour which precedes great sacrifices is one of agitation and agony, he no longer keeps before Christian's eyes, as formerly, thoughts of detachment and strength of will,—no, he whispers gently to him only Our Lord's wish to His disciples: *Pax vobis.* Peace, peace, it is the desired refuge of the faithful soul when temptation assails and its own weakness terrifies it. Later on, when Christian will have taken his place among the Levites, Just will know well how to recover the energy of his accents; he will aid his brother's soul in ascending the steep heights of perfection, himself depriving him sometimes of even the most legitimate consolations, such as the happiness of seeing him (Just) often, and of thus profiting by the last months of their being together. Now he thinks only of putting Christian's heart at ease.

It is peace too which he wishes his mother; but he does so in a language more austere, knowing that she is capable of bearing it. Whilst her husband and Christian are travelling, this generous woman on the eve of giving to God her second and last child, seeks strength and consolation in a retreat. Just congratulates her thereupon.

"Our Lord Himself leads you," he says, "in placing in your hands the Exercises of St. Ignatius. There is nothing more to say to you now except that you must read and act accordingly. This life is indeed a thorny path, but nevertheless, to set you the example, Our Lord did not hesitate to walk therein. Would you shrink from following Him? ... *Above all, preserve your soul in peace;* do not let yourself be troubled by anything you may be told or that may be done around you. One thing alone is essential—to love God. *Pray unceasingly: I am convinced that it is this especially Our Lord requires of you.* And words are not necessary: it is the heart that prays. Moreover, we must not pray for the sake of the joy we find in prayer; we must love God alone, and even when it seems to bring us nothing in return. "May the peace of Our Lord be ever with you, my very dear mother, and may He grant you the grace to be all His even to your last hour! Adieu, my good mother."

Another time he writes to her: "You must find yourself somewhat lonely; but St. John the Baptist will teach you that the more one is separated from men, and at the moment when he believes himself the most alone, then is he the least so. They only who have not given themselves to God find themselves isolated when cut off from conversation with men. For the true Christian it is indeed the contrary. All know this in theory, but very few attempt to test it in practice. *Mistrusting the boundless goodness of divine Providence*, they fear to rely too much upon it, and seek support and consolation elsewhere.

"Silence in God's presence is the first condition for entering upon the spiritual life. *You are well situated to advance in this path.* If you accustom yourself to habits of introspection several times a day, you will soon be able to practise this, even when speaking to others, or when engaged at your ordinary duties. And finally, after the example of many saints, this living ever in God's presence will become habitual to you, and constitute your greatest happiness. Then scarcely anything can trouble you, which is not always the case with you now.

"Adieu, my dear mother. I say all this to you without knowing why. Select from it only what strikes you as suited to your needs."

The vacations were over, and Just had taken his brother to

the seminary at Issy. Both were going to enter upon a
retreat. Just at the moment when he is about to seek
retirement, there to taste the delights of union with God,
the elder thinks of the trials that may perhaps await the
younger, during these first days of solitude; and he hastens
to send him these lines breathing the ardor of an apostle,
the tenderness of a mother: "Do not be astonished, my
dear one, at receiving these few words from me. If I write
so soon after leaving you it is only to tell you once more not
to be frightened and discouraged during this retreat and
your first days at the seminary, should the demon seek to
prove you by temptations of weariness and of regret for
the past. Let it not trouble you. Do you not wish to do
everything for love of God? Offer Him, then, all your trials
as an oblation which will rejoice His paternal heart. Strive
to be joyous no matter what contradictions and vexations
beset you.

"And now, my dear one, give yourself entirely to God;
let your heart go out to Him—that heart which He craves
and which He entreats of you. Open it to grace, my dear
child, cast no glances back, forget the past; you are now
beginning the most beautiful portion of your life. I have
little experience, but I believe, nevertheless, that I do not
deceive myself in this matter.

"Pray also for me, my child; I have great need of prayer;
my only reliance is upon God's mercy."

We should like to lay before our readers all of Just's
subsequent letters to Christian. Now that this soul is
God's he desires it to be wholly His. No longer fearing
lest it be troubled, he boldly exhorts it to fervor. The following letter, which we quote almost entire, gives an idea of
the stamp which he sought to imprint upon this soul.

"You must not feel anxious, my dear one, if I do not
write to you oftener. And why should I write so often?

You will answer, 'You are two years older than I; you ought to instruct me.' But you have much nearer to you One Who knocks at your door every hour of the day, and Who asks nothing better than to instruct you, Who entreats you to listen to Him, and to keep yourself in silence in order to understand Him; for the voice of Jesus can be heard only in the silence of the heart.—Alas! both you and I have let years slip by, indeed, the whole of our lives, keeping ourselves far from the good Friend of our souls. But now for you as well as for me the happy hour has come which our Master marked out as the end of our estrangement from Him. And we are both, I hope, in His divine Presence, entreating Him to forget our past ingratitude, and to let our love henceforth be so much the more ardent in proportion to our lack of it heretofore. *Erravi sicut ovis quæ periit: quære servum tuum, quia mandata tua non sum oblitus.*

"What, then, shall be the object of our pursuit, or what shall we seek after save Him Who urges you and me to keep ourselves entirely for Him? And remember that we must reserve nothing, we must give no creature the least part of ourselves. It is to Our Lord we owe ourselves entire. All our affections should be for Him; even that which we bear to others should be referred to Him. This love for Him, should He grant us the grace to love Him, ought to master our every affection and thought, so that we neither desire nor will anything out of Him. Let us put forth all our efforts to obtain this love.

"Our nature always draws us down to creatures, and towards some it seems we are attracted in spite of ourselves, so great is the active affection which we bear them. And it is herein we must open our souls to grace, that they may be penetrated by its action. It is very easy to know whether the affection which we have for anyone comes from God or from nature; if from God, it does not disturb our

peace, we are calm, and that person's absence causes us no
anxiety; whilst, on the other hand, anxiety and perturba-
tion are proof that it is the flesh and not the spirit that
speaks.

"Attach yourself, then, my dear one, to none but Our
Lord; everything else is only a means of going to Him,
and should be used for that purpose. Should the occasion
present itself of conversing with some one about God, as
sometimes happens (and one knows in the depths of his
heart when such is the case), take advantage of it as a
means which God Himself offers to draw you towards Him,
and thank Him for it. If such occasions be lacking, what
then must you do? Our Lord will supply something else:
He is not a slave to means, and He will always accomplish
His end. The sum of our duty is to be indifferent to all
things, and to desire only what God wishes, keeping ourselves in peace, and laboring to become, by the help of God's
grace, humble and filled with love for Him. . . ."

Some time after, in the month of November, 1863, when
he had already been called to the deaconate, he completes
in a little note this beautiful lesson of detachment. He
writes: "I cannot go out next Wednesday, as you desire.
. . . Understand, moreover, that on the eve of an ordination it would be unbecoming for us to be seen walking
through the town without necessity. Upon a little consideration you will think as I do on this point, even if it
should not strike you at first.

"Within the next fortnight I will make you a call of
about half an hour; this will be sufficient for whatever
serious matter we may wish to talk about, and we should not
spend too much time in the mere enjoyment of each other's
society—it is useless. I greatly prefer to this that you
make a little visit to the Blessed Sacrament, or a spiritual
reading; and it will be far more profitable to you.

"Would you like to attend the ordination? If so, I will obtain the necessary permission for you. Do not attach yourself too much to things of this sort, for all such consolations are mere vanity, and it appears to me that you could spend this time more advantageously in silence and recollection."

With his parents he, of course, tempered somewhat this bluntness of language; yet even in speaking or writing to them he loses no opportunity of preparing them for the grand sacrifice, at one time telling them in an off-hand way the news of the missionaries in the extreme East—their adventures, shipwrecks, martyrdom, etc.; or, another time, leaving the parlor often a few minutes, to take part in some meeting appointed by his charity or zeal. Occasionally he proffers them a little instruction in his letters, veiling austerity of doctrine under gayety of expression. "The few days that we have to spend on earth," he writes, "will soon pass; and oh! how joyful will be that meeting in heaven, where we may love one another in Our Lord without disquietude, without the least fear of ever again being separated. No doubt, dear father, you will call me a friar preacher again; but if you think that is going to close my mouth, you are surely mistaken, for I feel so deeply the importance of these spiritual matters that I cannot forego alluding to them. It has been a long time, hasn't it? since you told me that I was a man of fixed ideas; I admit that I am, and I now add that I have one idea more fixed than all other fixed ideas in the world, namely, that there will soon come a day without end, in which you will exult with joy at not having made of your two boys gallant cavaliers, but, please God, good fathers of families. For with all due deference to you, let me say that Christian and I look forward to nothing less than becoming the head of a family, but of a kind that gives one no trouble of house-keeping."

A few days after this, congratulating his father on his feast-day, he writes: "I hope, dear father, that the good St. Edmund will obtain for you what is so necessary in your present position—perfect resignation to all that the good God asks of you. You will probably say, dear father, that I am ambitious when I tell you that I desire for you nothing so much as that you become a saint. I do not know how to tell you what is necessary to be a saint; for, as you have justly remarked to me, I have not yet the authority to preach, consequently, I lack the graces appertaining thereto. I can only lay bare to you my thoughts, asking you to take my words for what they are worth."

It was in these dispositions of fervor and zeal that Just prepared for his ordination to the deaconate. It took place during the Ember days of Advent, in the church of St. Sulpice. On that memorable day Mgr. Darboy, unable to stand the fast, fell exhausted in the midst of the ordination of the priests, that of the deacons being accomplished. After this, the Seminary of the Missions always had its ordinations in its own chapel, and it was here that Just was made a priest.

There now remained but six months between him and the great day. He thought of nothing else; his union with Our Lord became continual, his piety more effective and more tender. It seems as if the grand work of voluntary death had been accomplished; life was now overflowing, but it was a hidden life the secret of which he guards for his communications with God. Only his brethren in the apostolate, especially the most fervent, and some friends outside, initiated into his sentiments, discover anything of this. Even to the few favored ones whose visits he still consents to receive, he has little to say, and he has an abstracted air as of one who does violence to himself in breaking off an interior conversation which is evidently interrupted by creatures. Also with his brethren he speaks little; but his words, always simple and ordinary in expression, coming from the depths of his heart, go straight to one's soul. When they ask of him counsel or encouragement, he recollects himself a moment ere replying, "as if," says one of his fellow-students, "consulting some one whose words he interprets." When the duty either of study or charity does not call him elsewhere, he is sure to be found before the Blessed Sacrament: there he spends hours at a time, especially during their free days at Meudon, and sometimes even in his visits, for example, when he goes to see his cousin, recently received into the novitiate of the Brothers of St. Vincent de Paul at Chaville. The community of the Seminary of the Missions descends to the chapel for morning prayer at half-past five o'clock, but Just, always up at four, is a few minutes after in the gallery, and he has already prayed more than an hour and a quarter when the usual meditation begins. Daily he receives Holy Communion with angelic piety, and hears an entire Mass in thanksgiving. His day's work commences, then, with three hours and more of mental prayer. During breviary, which they recite in common, such is his recollection that one of the missionaries declares that he has no better means of re-animating his devotion than of casting his eyes towards the stall where Just is chanting.

A letter which he writes to his brother on Good Friday reveals something of the ardor inflaming him. He says: "Ah! how beautiful yesterday and to-day, indeed all these days of Holy Week! How one can plunge himself (if we may use such an expression here) in Jesus, and be immersed in Him! One becomes a madman, yes, my dear one, a madman, in presence of these mysteries of love, be-

ing oblivious of everything else except to adore with transports, to adore unceasingly, thus beginning his heaven on
earth in a most admirable commingling of sweetness and
bitterness. . . . Cultivate love in your heart, my dear one;
seek it in solitude; listen not to those voices which tell you
that love belongs to that other life; no, it is for this also,
and true life is that of love. . . . Let love be the principle of
all your actions."

Love on earth is often associated with sadness, because
here it is an exile; but its real nature is to produce joy,
and when deeply felt, exuberant joy.   Easter is come.
Christian is called to the tonsure at the same time that Just
is called to the priesthood. The elder brother's heart pours itself out in that of the younger, in hearing of this double happiness.   "We must love joyfully," he writes, "since it is
by obedience you advance.   Say, then, with all your heart:
*Lætatus sum in his quæ dicta sunt mihi: in domum Domini
ibimus.*   Doubtless, we should bear ever in mind the
thought of our past and present wretchedness, to keep us
from presumption; but let not this sentiment predominate
over our joy in anticipation of the marvels which are so
soon to be wrought in us.   Yes, joy should fill our hearts
and keep them in profound peace, since we are privileged
children, and repose in the arms of Jesus, Who Himself nour-
ishes, vivifies, sustains and fills us.   Alleluia!   Yes, the
sentiment of our wretchedness and the salutary fear which
it inspires should indeed pale before the rays of that sun
which is rising in the east, to enkindle in us the fire of divine
love.   Act more from love than from fear, act from love
only.   It is with our eyes fixed ever on the Source of
love that we must advance; and then the years are nothing, it matters not whether we have been long in God's
service or but a little while, for the sight of Jesus, so
beautiful, so amiable, detaches the heart from all cre-

ated things, to unite it inseparably to Him, its Saviour.

"However, let us understand that this love does not consist in feeling. We should make so little account of consolations of this sort as never to be the least troubled for a moment when deprived of them. You have doubtless learned this in reading the life of St. Teresa, and also, perhaps, from the writings of St. John of the Cross, which writings I now recommend to you. You love Jesus when nothing can turn you away from Him, when you love nothing except in and for Him, and when you are willing to make every sacrifice for His sake, not only as regards material necessities, but also of the intelligence and heart."

Thus, wholly in bondage to the sweet and powerful operations of divine love, this holy young man would have isolated himself entirely from creatures; but zeal is the activity of love, and when it commands, the loving soul joyfully sacrifices its repose. It is at this epoch, the spring of 1864, that a new work is offered him: to the apostolate of the quarries is added that among the workmen of a capsule factory at Sèvres. The majority of these, being Germans, were completely isolated, by their language and habits, amid a suburban population. A few of the more elderly and more Christian of their number had some ascendancy over the others, and endeavored to keep alive in their midst the thoughts and desires inspired by faith. But they needed the succors of religion. Just, familiar with the German tongue, made their acquaintance, with a view to the good of their souls; and his repeated applications in their behalf at length succeeded in obtaining for them the spiritual care of one of the community of St. Vincent de Paul from Grenelle, to prepare them for the Paschal duty. This good work, initiated by our candidate, was continued for several years.

At the same time, and actuated by the same zeal, he labored unceasingly, sparing himself neither pains nor trouble, to withdraw from vice some young men who were greatly exposed to temptation. On these occasions, no longer avaricious of his time, nor jealous of his solitude as formerly, he multiplied his talks, called to his aid his parents and friends from without, and gave himself no rest until the desired result was obtained, or, at least, until he had exhausted all the artifices which charity could inspire to bring about such results.

The ordination was approaching, and a last trial would complete in this fervent lover of the cross his resemblance to Jesus crucified. His venerable parents, whom at the hour of the final separation we shall see models of heroic resignation, were now passing through that period of agony which preceded the grand sacrifice, and they could not but feel that weakness of nature which Our Saviour Himself willed to experience for our consolation. M. de Bretenières, especially, suffered most keenly as the moment of immolation drew nigh. In the midst of that obscurity in which trouble envelops the afflicted soul, it seemed to him, at times, that Just, mistaken in his ideas of duty, had entered upon the wrong path, thus rashly exposing himself to a thousand dangers, even risking his soul (for the apostolic vocation, alas! is not exempt from spiritual peril); and wrung with anguish, he was tempted to look upon it as a useless cruelty in regard to those whom it sacrificed, and really prejudicial to the missionary himself; hence his bitter complaints, his reproaches, sombre predictions, his conversations steeped in sorrow. To these assaults of paternal tenderness overwhelmed by distress Just opposed that gentle and peaceful firmness which lay in the depths of his nature, and constituted his virtue's strength. But oh! what concealed sufferings for his filial heart! How afflicting to him must not have been these interviews with his parents! Truly, it was for him also the agony preceding his Calvary![1]

We give this on the authority of his cousin, then a novice at Chaville, whom he made a confidant of his anguish. From this same witness we here quote a picture of Just's soul, at the time when the sacerdotal unction is about to fortify the champion for the struggles of the apostolate.

"As to holiness," he says, "Just was not a man of reasoning, of analysis, of theory; . . .his was not a discursive sanctity. The gift which he had received from God was of the highest order. There was in his spirit and heart a formidable principle of renunciation which he always applied with habitual resolution, and which gave to his whole life, by a unique impression, that seal of sanctity remarked by all who knew him at this epoch. . . . How was it that he attained so young that degree of grace which is the prerogative only of such of God's servants as have been long in His service and well tried therein? How had he suddenly reached the summit of the spiritual life, making of sanctity a vast synthesis, the starting point of which is, *Crucifige te ipsum?* I know not : his confessor is the person best fitted to judge hereon; but I will say this, that I believe his was a nature

---

[1] In recalling these painful circumstances, we do not believe ourselves guilty of the least disrespect to the memory of a father venerable for his virtues. The following shows in what touching language M. de Bretenières himself confirms our words. The quotation is from his *Souvenirs sur mon fils* (Souvenirs of my Son). He says : " For a long time Just strove to familiarize us with the thoughts of the parting hour which must soon sound; for a long time his sacrifice had been made, and he wished us to share it. . . . I believed it a duty sometimes to cite the commandments as opposed to his designs, and to say severe things to him in this connection. He received it all with that gentle deference habitual to him, and which we, in our blindness, attributed to a sort of insensibility, inexplicable to us, alas!

"Thus I tortured my dear child, without ever suspecting that at that very time (a fact revealed subsequently in his letters) his heart was full of the deepest compassion for what he called *his poor father's grief.* In this expressed proof of his filial affection (which I never doubted, however) there is that which will bring tears from my eyes to my dying day."

extraordinarily good, or, to express it differently, a nature having extraordinarily few imperfections; that the gifts of grace were very abundantly bestowed upon it from the beginning, and that the soul's baptismal innocence was preserved,—all which wonderfully assisted its flight towards God. . . . I know that he studied St. John of the Cross a great deal. . . . In fact, he walked in the way traced out by the famous canticle of *The Dark Night;* and I believe it was thus he found great holiness without any of those reasonings, reflections, strategies, taught by writers on spirituality, and which we, altogether different from him, find so helpful to our progress. What I have just said reminds me of an expression of St. Vincent de Paul, who having reached the grand and unique formula of Christian perfection, wrote thus to a pious soul: 'Oh! how little it takes to be a saint !'

" I also believe that Just's prayer was very probably that of contemplation, at least during the last two years of his life, if not longer."

This vigorous sketch accords with the opinion of all who were best acquainted with our aspirant at this time, which opinion one of his brethren expresses as follows: " Father de Bretenières' is so grand a soul that I hope God will one day allow him to be canonized, even should He not deign to grant him the crown of martyrdom."

To describe Just's feelings at the approach of ordination, we make a last extract from his own written correspondence, and also from his brother's recollections.

He writes to M. Rabardelle, a missionary in Siam: " I now, especially by reason of my disposition, a little rough, as you well know, live somewhat like a hermit, talking with all comers on all sorts of subjects except that which most engrosses my thoughts. And although I feel in the depths of my heart a secret need of another soul to whom I can unbosom myself, I find none. Nevertheless, I am far from complaining of this spiritual solitude, as it were: it is really a great blessing to have no one but Our Lord for witness of what passes in the heart. And how could I complain of anything, when in six weeks I shall have the happiness of offering the Holy Sacrifice? I feel the joy that is pouring in upon me from all sides, but I do not know whether I should yield to it. I should not hesitate to do so, were it not for some recollections of my past life, strikingly in contrast to all that now fills my soul! *De stercore erigens pauperem.* . . . Nevertheless, I believe that peace and joy predominate, despite so many interior storms. And soon I shall offer Our Lord in sacrifice! Oh! what folly for me to think of such a thing!—I who am so far from being prepared!. . . Yet, in spite of all this, *laus, honor, jubilatio, gloria Deo nostro Jesus!* Praise Him for me, and in my name, for all the excesses of grace with which He has filled me.''

The following souvenir from his brother relates to the last walk they took together preceding the retreat for ordination: '' When at Meudon, Just greatly preferred solitary walks in the woods to finding recreation in those little diversions so enjoyable to some of his brethren. ' He was very fond of retiring to a secluded spot amidst a thick copse. It had been pointed out to him by a pious missionary, himself much attached to the place. After this latter's departure, Just continued to frequent what he called his hermitage, spending nearly the whole day [2] there, meditating at the

---

[1] He afterwards regretted as a species of selfishness this having kept himself so much apart from his brethren at this time ; and he counselled those whom he left behind him at the seminary to join in the evening recreations at Meudon, more from charity than preference, and without losing recollection.

[2] It appears that even the days did not suffice : and more than once during the vacations he was known to repair thither in the night to pray, to exercise himself in the *bivouac* of the missionary, to inure himself to the dampness of the night, to the darkness, to the forest noises,—to all that the apostle must confront in his rude existence, which in hardships is so often that of an outlaw.

One morning, one of his brethren, having risen at dawn, surprised him at prayer

foot of a little cross which he had set up.¹ Four days before we both entered retreat, he in preparation for ordination to the priesthood, I to receive tonsure, he took me to
his little solitude. I cannot attempt to reproduce his conversation, but I will say that it was imbued with such extraordinary suavity, peacefulness, and at the same time
strength and energy, as I can never forget. Just's soul lay
open before me, revealing alternately the pure, sweet joy,
inundating the heart of the new priest, and the vigorous
aspirations of the missionary. . . .This was the last intimate
conversation I was ever to have with my brother on earth.
After he had given me some excellent advice in regard to
my future ministry, dwelling strongly upon the necessity
of absolute detachment, we both fell on our knees before
the little cross and prayed together for the missions, especially for that one to which he would so soon be assigned
by his superiors."

Ere entering the retreat for ordination, Just begged his
brother and his parents to protect his solitude by sparing
him all visitors. His retreat was one continual prayer; he
seldom quitted the chapel or the gallery, where one beheld
him, ever on his knees, absorbed in meditation. What
passed between God and his soul at that time remains his
own secret.

At last, on the 21st of May, 1864, in the chapel of the

in the woods, on his knees, and so profoundly recollected, that he was all unconscious
of the rabbits playing around him. Just was too faithful an observer of the rule to
quit the house thus at night without permission. His superior, knowing the vigor
of his soul, had authorized him to follow its attraction.

¹ We think this is also the spot where, finding himself one day with one of his
most fervent co-laborers in the work of the quarries, Just asked him to consent to
represent, for a moment, all the poor quarrymen. Then, kneeling before him with
a true humility far removed from all savor of affectation, Just asked pardon for
whatever bad example he had ever given these workmen, and for all the proud
thoughts he had ever had in visiting them.

After his departure, his brethren, wishing to preserve this little hermitage in
memory of Just, cut a cross on the bark of the tree at the foot of which he had
knelt. The spot became later a pilgrim shrine for the aspirants.

Missions, with ten of his brethren, he received the imposition of hands from Mgr. Thomine Dezmazures, Vicar Apostolic of Thibet. Christian at the same time received tonsure in the church of St. Sulpice. Their parents assisted at the elder son's ordination, but respecting his desire for solitude, they withdrew after the ceremony without asking to see him, and the new priest passed the whole day in prayer.

On Monday, feast of the Holy Trinity, he celebrated his first Mass, in a chapel of the seminary, assisted by the venerable pastor of St. Peter's of Châlon, who had baptized him; his brother and his former preceptor serving it. His parents and a few friends were present. One of these latter exclaimed on retiring, "I have just heard Mass in Paradise!"

Just would have preferred remaining alone with God, but after a sufficient length of time for him to make a proper thanksgiving, his brother sought him and requested that he would give his benediction to the assistants. Answering by a look which seemed to say, *It is good for us to be here,* he, nevertheless, arose in silence, and blessed those who were awaiting him. When they had kissed his hands, he immediately retired to his dear solitude.

The preparation of the missionary was finished: three years of heroic labor had made of him an apostle; there now remained for him but to consummate the sacrifice.

CHAPTER IV.

THE DEPARTURE.—THE VOYAGE.—SOJOURN IN MANTCHOORIA.—ARRIVAL IN COREA (1864-1865).

THREE weeks elapsed between the ordination of the new priests and the day on which they were apprised of their respective apostolic destinations. During all this time Just seemed to think of nothing but the happiness of being a priest. He celebrated Mass, sometimes in a little chapel of the Rue du Regard, sometimes in the church (then the parish church) of the Missions, where his parents could assist at it. The remainder of the day he spent in acts of thanksgiving. His prayer was almost continual: he even arose in the night to pray. On one such occasion, being in company with one of his brethren, their transports of joy were so great, that with a sudden interruption of their prayer they both prostrated themselves to recite the *Te Deum.* We were told this by M. Bon, missionary to western Tonquin, who knew more than one secret of Just's soul.

What henceforth ceased to be a secret to any was the ardent desire for martyrdom which had taken possession of Just's heart. Many of his former brethren have written to us that he never made known this desire before his ordination to the priesthood, his humility leading him to fear there was something of pride in aspiring so high. This assertion, truthful in the main, needs modification. In 1862, writing to his former preceptor and acquainting him with the death of a missionary massacred in China for the Faith, despite the treaties, Just adds as if in joyful accents, "So you perceive that martyrdom here is not entirely a thing of the past." Again we learn that a certain candidate, having yielded to discouragement and recoiled before the missionary vocation, Just made every effort to re-animate his courage, though without avail; and, when in a last interview the young man thanked him warmly for his tender charity, Just said to him, "Will you do something for me?" —"Oh! with all my heart!" was the answer.—"Well, then," replied Just, "when you pray, ask for me the grace of a double martyrdom."

These last words, which are perfectly authenticated, seem

to us undeniable proof that Just aspired to the supreme sacrifice, ere he had attained the priesthood. However, up to the time of his ordination the humble candidate was timid in his indulgence of this generous desire. But from the day on which he first offered the blood of Jesus Christ this timidity vanished, he could restrain himself no longer. Our Lord Himself had implanted the aspiration in his heart, and the divine action is so evident that he does not dream of withdrawing from it. Doubtless it is this which occupied him in those long communications with the divine Master. Never once did he offer the Holy Sacrifice without asking the grace of mingling his blood with that of the Saviour. This we have on the authority of his own letters to some of his most intimate friends, scattered about on the various missions,—which confidence they have revealed since his death. One of them, M. Dubernard, a missionary in Thibet, writes thus to Mme. de Bretenières: "We often spoke of martyrdom. This dear soul deemed itself unworthy of asking this grace. '*I am not of the wood of which martyrs are made,*' he would say; '*martyrdom requires that its victims be innocent, and you know what I am.*' But scarcely has he descended from the altar for the first time, when his language is very different. '*Ask for martyrdom,*' he writes to me; 'it is God's will that we implore this favor. Is it not the prayer which we daily address Him after the *Memento* for the dead, when we ask Him to let us form part of the company of the holy apostles and martyrs?' "

At last the day arrived when our aspirants were to become missionaries. The Society of Foreign Missions is a congregation the members of which are not bound to it by vows; each one is always at liberty to leave, yet remaining therein, he practises religious obedience all his life. Hence, up to the last moment, the aspirants are in complete ignorance of the field of labor to which they are assigned, this being decided by the council of directors after much deliberation, studying the respective needs of each mission, the qualifications of each subject.

On this point Just was perfectly indifferent. He was not of the number of those who make half sacrifices; and having renounced his will in the whole, once for all, he had no desire to follow it in details. When acquainted with his destination, he manifested great joy, which several of his brethren attributed to the fact of this mission being a particularly perilous one; but when interrogated hereon by one of his most intimate confidants, he declared that he really had no preferences, and that he rejoiced when apprised of his destination because this knowledge was to him the expression of God's will in his regard,—Heaven, by the voice of obedience, had selected him a spouse, wherefore he loved her.

At the end of a conversation with the Father Superior on the 13th of June, the latter said in a playful manner to him, " Suppose I tell you now your mission field? "—" I am ready, Father," replied Just.—" Where would you prefer being sent? "—" I have no choice."—" Well, then, I will send you to Thibet."—" Very well, Father."—" No, you shall go to Tonquin."—" Admirable."—" No; I mean to send you to China."—" Just as you please."—" Now, let us speak seriously," said M. Albrand suddenly, his countenance becoming grave.—" Ah! if you are in earnest, Father, that is another thing," said the young man, falling on his knees, "let me listen to your words as to God's commands."—" You are going to Corea."—" It is what I should have chosen," replied Just, and he immediately withdrew.

It was now indeed the new missionary's joy burst forth. He says, " I believe that Our Lord has given me the better

part; for just at present this is one of our best, if not indeed the very best of our missions,—one of those where it
is easiest to spend one's self for Jesus' sake. Corea forever, land of martyrs! True, just now there is no open persecution there, but sweat replaces blood. There is so
much work that one is worn out by it."

Here, then, was the secret of Just's joy. But he did not
triumph alone; three of his brethren, MM. Beaulieu, Dorie, and Huin were appointed to the same mission. They,
too, like himself, were destined to receive the crown of martyrdom. One of them, M. Dorie, was not at first told the
country to which he was going, but merely that he would
be with Just. His joy at this was so great that he went
about the house saying to all whom he met, " Oh! what
happiness for me! I am with Father de Bretenières!"

After returning thanks to God, Just began immediately
to occupy himself with his mission, studying everything relating to Corea, and, with calm foresight, making all the
preparations for his departure. As to the latter, however, he
took no advantage of his personal situation to increase his
resources and means of action. On the contrary, never did
his spirit of poverty and love of detachment shine forth
more brilliantly than now; and of this we will soon adduce
some touching proofs. But he charged himself with providing for his companions' wants as well as his own, procuring all such articles as were strictly necessary for travellers, and also those useful to the missionary. He asked his
mother to regard his three companions as her sons, knowing that their families were poor and unable to assist them
pecuniarily. Said one of them, " He put all in common
between us, even his mother's purse." *The four Coreans,*
as they were called, were one in heart and soul. They
were often seen praying together, or talking among
themselves. Each had promised the others to accept what

could be shared by all four, with the exception of money,
and this they would not hear mentioned.

Once the poor mother thought she had succeeded in
making her son accept a souvenir. Possessing a relic of
the true Cross, she offered it to Just. It was tempting to
his piety; he accepted the relic and had it transferred to a
new reliquary to guard its authenticity, apparently filled
with joy at the possession of such a treasure. The delighted mother, going to Issy to see her second son, ac-
quaints him with the good news. " Ah!" said Christian,
" either I do not know my brother, or your present will
soon be returned to you." And his words were confirmed.
Mme. de Bretenières went direct from Issy to the Rue du
Bac. Just hastened to her at the first summons, holding the relic in his hand. " Mother, " said he, " I beg
you to take this back; I wish to possess nothing of my
own."

Such detachment would pass with some for lack of feeling, or harshness, if you will. They who judge thus
know not what is exacted of chosen souls by Him Who desires to be their only treasure. Our holy missionary's
mother was worthy of comprehending this exalted lesson.
Far from finding in her *Souvenirs,* from which we borrow
this anecdote, the least complaint of Just's conduct in this
respect, we there learn that from the day he knew of his
appointment to Corea he relaxed much of his former austerity towards his parents, and gladly accorded them all
the time at his disposal. He had them assist at his Mass,
he consented to receive their visits frequently, he charged
them with his material preparations for departure, wishing
thereby to distract them from their grief, and also to associate them in the merit of his sacrifice. He even allowed
himself to be photographed, which he had heretofore always refused, and he gave these photographs, enriched by

his signature, to various of his friends. He accorded his parents a whole day at their apartments in Paris—a day precious indeed, but really very painful, notwithstanding his freedom of spirit and his sprightly simplicity, which even here did not fail him. Another time he took his brother to Meudon to spend the entire day (a holiday) with him. But although now making himself so accessible to his dear parents, he was equally anxious to avoid all other visitors, and even begged his father and his brother to keep them away. "If you only knew," he would say, "the great need one has of living with God at such a time as this!" Finally, during the week preceding the departure, feeling drawn to profound recollection, he obtains his parents' consent to his request that they, too, will refrain from coming to see him during the few days' retreat just before he leaves. "God will reward you a thousand-fold," he writes to his mother, "for the sacrifice you make in thus allowing me to remain, as far as possible under the circumstances, in solitude, to prepare myself for the departure." Such is the spirit of the saints; exterior actions are of little account in their eyes; it is the interior they regard. To go to the ends of the earth, it is not this that occupies their thoughts; no, to them the one thing essential is to watch ever over their hearts, that they may keep the first place for God.

The 15th of July had come—the day fixed upon for the departure. M. and Mme. de Bretenières came that morning to assist at the Mass for the community, celebrated by Just in the seminary chapel. In appointing him to say this Mass, the venerable Superior had thus responded to a secret desire of many of Just's fellow-students who longed to receive Communion from his hand at the moment of separation. We here borrow M. de Bretenières' account of the last parting; it is expressed in language unsur-

passed for its simple and pathetic grandeur. He says:
" We went to the Rue du Bac at six o'clock in the morning, and received from our child's hands that divine Food which alone could give us strength to sustain the last farewells. Oh! how shall I speak of the emotions that filled our whole being! what heart breakings! And yet in offering my son for immolation I have always sought alleviation of my grief in the thought that Providence may some day bring him back to us to close our eyes.

" After Mass we went to the parlor, where Just soon joined us. The conversation was not long. We were standing, like travellers who meet one another on the road, and merely exchange a few words ere parting. We had restrained our emotions so far, but the least word or circumstance would have overcome us. We knelt to receive his last blessing, then pressing him to my heart I tore myself from his arms....Thanks be to God ! Our farewells had been such as those of Christians should be—without violent outbursts, without tears."

Mme. de Bretenières, in her notes, recurs to her husband's account and adds only these words: " Day of sad, sad remembrance! That on which I was informed of his martyrdom, with the certainty of his eternal happiness, was certainly less painful to me."

The ceremony attendant upon the departure of the missionaries took place in the evening. There are few of our readers who have not assisted, once at least, at this touching solemnity. Just, dreading the effect upon his parents, his father especially, gently and respectfully counselled them not to come, also, not to accompany him to the depot. They came, however, but took a place in the gallery, and did not approach their son.

A few minutes before the ceremony, a friend from Dijon went to Just's cell to see him. He found the missionary very calm. "Pray for me," said Just, "yes, pray, pray, that I may obtain what I desire."

And this desire was undoubtedly martyrdom. At four o'clock the community assembled in the garden at the foot of a statue venerated as Our Lady, Queen of martyrs. Here the candidates and the missionaries sang the litanies and the *Hymn of Departure* which Gounod had composed for the occasion. Just's countenance, very pale a moment before, now grew radiant with color and animation, his brightening eyes and his clear, ringing voice attracting the attention of the spectators, many of whom made the remark that his expression was one of heavenly joy.

The missionaries that were to leave were ten in number. Entering the church, they ranged themselves, standing, on the altar steps, whilst the choir chanted this verse of the psalm: *Quam speciosi pedes evangelizantium pacem, evangelizantium bona!* "How beautiful are the feet of them who bear good tidings, the evangel of peace!" At the same time all the candidates, and the men in the aisle, came forward to kneel before them, kiss their feet, and then rising, embrace them.

Just stood on the Epistle side; his carriage was firm and erect, his arms were crossed and his eyes raised to heaven with an expression of angelic serenity. Writes a person who was present: "On his radiant face one read rather the joys of a return than grief at departure." To each of his friends, on embracing him, he said some words of affection and asked for prayers. It seems to me in writing these lines that I still feel his blessed embrace. When Christian had kissed his brother's feet, Just raised him up, and pressed him to his heart, saying with a smile as he did so, "Courage, courage; often recall my words, Jesus in the Most Holy Sacrament! Jesus forever!" Adds Christian in his Souvenirs, "I knew that during this time my father and my mother made aloud together the sacrifice of their son to God, and recited the *Te Deum.* It was the triumph of grace over nature. The ceremony was over, the crowd dispersed. In passing through the seminary again, I once more caught sight of Just. He was surrounded by a throng. I extended my hand to him; he pressed it, saying, ' Adieu, it is over,' with a look that seemed to tell me heaven would be our next meeting-place."

Let us listen for a last time to our martyr's father. He says: " We descended from the gallery where we had made the last sacrifice. The omnibus, which was to take the missionaries to the station, was in the yard. Some few persons remained, desirous of participating in all the emotions of this day. Should we remain also? We hesitated: the mother would have remained, but the father thought it wiser quietly to withdraw. We returned to our abode in silence, absorbed in our thoughts."

Love of poverty signalized the missionaries' last moments at the seminary. Immediately before starting, Just found two sous in a drawer: he gave them to one of his brethren; M. Dorie found five sous in his pocket: he gave them to the poor. " What happiness!" exclaimed Just, as he joyfully entered the vehicle; " for more than twenty years I have longed to be poor, and now I am really so at last."

We are indebted to an excellent priest who had known Just since his birth for some details of the first part of the journey—that from Paris to Marseilles. The Abbé Pataille, then pastor of a parish church in the diocese of Dijon, feeling called to solitude, was about to repair to the Grande Chartreuse for the purpose of deciding his vocation. Having learned in time the date of the missionaries' departure, he advanced his journey eight days in order to join them at Beaune. He accompanied them as far as Lyons, spending the time in conversation with Just, who could not recover from his astonishment that any one should so inconvenience himself to see him. At the Perrache station, in Lyons, just at the parting moment, M. Pataille confided to the missionary the secret of his (M. Pataille's) vocation. The signal for departure suddenly put an end to the conversation, and the worthy pastor withdrew, without once looking back, and with his face buried in his handkerchief, to conceal his emotion. He goes to Fourvières, and there the recollection of the calm heroism which he had just witnessed triumphs over his last doubts. He too, like Just, is to offer himself in sacrifice; his is not a bloody sacrifice; but one nevertheless very hard to nature—the martyrdom of all his days. Under the name of Didier he will edify the Chartreuse; and when the hour of complete immolation by the perpetual vow arrives for him, he will suddenly feel all those interior pains, all that bitterness of sacrifice, the aridity of a soul more overcome than attracted, give place to that serenity and joy which are here a foretaste of the eternal reward. This transformation will be wrought during the first week of March, 1866; and some months afterwards the solitary will learn that the days which had seen his desolation of soul cease were for his holy friend those of a grand combat and triumph. [1]

The missionaries passed three days at Marseilles; pious pilgrimages to Notre Dame de la Garde, walks on the lonely rocks bordering the coast, "where one can silently meditate," writes Just, an excursion on the sea made in such stormy weather and with such fearlessness as astonished the master of the vessel—such was the manner in which our travellers spent their time whilst waiting for the ship to sail. At last, on the 19th of July, at three o'clock, the loosed moorings delivered the *Said* to the waves which

[1] Just consummated his martyrdom on the 8th of March, 1866.

were going to separate these young men forever from all that they had loved best on earth.

The sky was clear, but the violent wind bespoke for our new navigators a rough apprenticeship to the sea. However, on the morning of the 20th, notwithstanding the rolling of the ship, one of them said Mass, one of his companions holding the chalice and two others the tapers. Three times a day the missionaries assembled at the stern to sing canticles and hymns. Among the acquaintances they made were two young Protestant men, missionaries on their way to Canton. "Poor ministers!" writes Just to his parents, "they come near to us when we sing a hymn to the Blessed Virgin, they observe us when we recite our Office. I see them promenading the deck whilst we assemble together to converse concerning our hopes and our missions. This picture reminds me forcibly of the Catholic Church (here represented by ourselves), calm and united, and the Protestant sects, swayed by every wind of doctrine, as says St. Paul in speaking of the errors of his time. We asked them concerning their plans at Quang Tong—what establishments they had founded there, and what conversions Anglicanism had made there. They could give us no information on the subject. Receiving high salaries, they go to China, to scatter Bibles by the thousand and make a fortune, hoping some day to return to Europe, rich in money and praises, and there spend the rest of their lives in happiness, or what the world calls happiness. Decidedly, it is we who have chosen the better part."

The vessel touched at Messina; thence they took passage for Alexandria. The Suez canal not yet being opened, it was necessary to cross Egypt by rail, and at the other extremity of the isthmus embark a third time. The trains from Alexandria to Cairo bear little resemblance to those luxurious cars carrying pleasure-seekers to fashionable resorts. Crowded in cars scarcely covered, scorched by the July sun and the reflection from the desert, devoured by mosquitoes—it was thus our missionaries were initiated into the trials of the life they would henceforth lead. But their gayety is unimpaired; and the animation of youth allied to the inspirations of piety suggests to them a picturesque excursion which will make an interesting souvenir of their sojourn at Cairo. Here they were to pass but twenty-four hours. The day was spent in a ride on donkey-back to the grand mosque of Cairo. Many were the falls of first one and then another of our travellers during this ride. It might well be supposed that the coming night would be devoted to a much needed rest; but Just thought otherwise, and disclosing his plans, seven of his nine companions wished to participate in them. We quote from a letter written at Suez the amiable instigator's own account of the expedition which he conducted. He says:

" I had read in the travels of Mgr. Guillemin that on his arrival at Cairo he went three leagues from the city, to an old tree which is, according to all the traditions of the country, that which sheltered the Blessed Virgin and St. Joseph in their flight into Egypt with the Infant Jesus.

" The problem to solve was this: our supper not being over until ten o'clock, and our Mass commencing at four o'clock next morning, how, in the meantime, to contrive to travel three leagues (or rather six leagues, going and returning), through an unknown country, guided by Arabs, probably no better than those that might waylay us on the road. Mentioning it to our hotel-keeper's son, a young man about twenty years of age, he expressed a wish to be of the party, at which I was much pleased, as he spoke Arabic, and could thus be very useful to us in communicating with our guides. With great difficulty he obtained

his mother's consent to his accompanying us. Another
addition to our party, making it ten in number, was a young
Indian physician, who had been educated in our college in
Pondicherry, and who was now travelling with us. He
himself proposed going with us, and we accepted his offer.
Just as the hour of ten was striking, mounting our beasts,
all fresh and strong for the journey, we started off at
a gallop, preceded by two young Arabs carrying lan-
terns, and followed by three or four others whose business
was to urge on those that lagged behind. Scarcely had we
got outside the walls of the city, when from the depths of
ten vigorous chests arose the notes of the *Ave Maris Stella*,
followed by the psalm, *In exitu Israel de Egypto*, the whole
in a decided tremor, by reason of our being well shaken
up by the motion of our animals. It would be impossible
to tell you all the turns and roundabout ways we had to
take through cemeteries, villages, and plantations that lay
between us and our destination. The narrow defiles were
numerous, and our donkeys, although there was room for
but one at a time to pass, would always dispute the passage
with one another, two or three often darting forward together. On our way thither we had but three or four falls
from our beasts, and these so trifling as to be scarce worthy
of mention. Our donkeys trotted and galloped along so well
that in an hour and three quarters we had cleared the distance between Cairo and our place of pilgrimage. We found
here numerous Arabs sitting up watching, and dogs even
more numerous keeping them company. I have neglected
telling you of the dogs of Cairo, that live in the streets,
day and night, filling the place of public scavengers. As
we left the city their voices were heard in a most formidable concert. As we approached the Virgin's tree, our ears
were greeted again in the same manner. Before entering
the garden in which this tree stands, we dismount; the

Arabs precede us with torches; and now surrounding the trunk of this venerable sycamore which had stood for centuries, we once again sang the *Ave Maris Stella*, and murmured some invocations. The Arabs were mute with astonishment. Whilst we were singing, one of them climbed the tree and broke off a large branch which he handed us. Each of our party plucked a few flowers and gathered a few seeds from it; and then we started for Cairo, but at even a more lively gait than we had come. It was midnight. The bright moon revealed the beauty of these magnificent gardens, in which we beheld palm-trees, bananas, and, above all, jasmines and sweet-scented plants, filling the air with perfume.

"Our return was signalized by innumerable falls. Let me state, at the beginning, that I was not of the number of the unfortunate ones who fell. One of the donkeys having attempted to jump over a torrent, not seeing clearly, missed reaching the other side, and rolled over to the bottom, his rider, however, remaining on the opposite side, cast there by the violence of the fall. The donkey showed no signs of life. Dismounting myself, I approached him; I pulled him by the tail, then by the head: he never budged. Finally we left him, and the moment he found he was out of danger, he started up and commenced to run. Both rider and beast had been only frightened, not hurt; they rejoined the band, and thus trotting, galloping, we reached our hotel about two o'clock in the morning. We were to rise at half-past three to celebrate our Masses. Notwithstanding, I had the courage to lie down. I slept an hour and a half, and at the appointed hour in the morning I was in the chapel of the Franciscans. At half-past seven we took the Suez railway, that miserable road which not only moves at a snail's pace, but can be made to stop anywhere for the sum of about eighteen cents. This evening we are in Suez, where

I end this letter.   We dine in a magnificent hotel, near the
port, to the sound of musical instruments and the voices
of singers, making a din horrible to hear, although the
performers think we are charmed.   For me, these are the
farewells of the civilization which we now leave behind us."

The travellers were going to find civilization again on the
Cambodge, a large packet boat of the imperial transportation company, on which they embarked at Suez on the
26th of July.   All the comforts of life one might have enjoyed on this vast ship, had not the insupportable heat of
the Red Sea, in the height of the dog days, afforded ample
occasion of suffering.   Just congratulates himself on this
in a letter to his parents.   "It is the very thing needed,"
he writes, "to prevent our becoming enervated by the easy,
luxurious life we lead on ship-board."

Barring the heat, the passage of the Red Sea was a pleasant one.   The *Cambodge* touched at Aden, and soon entered
the Indian Ocean, where our missionaries had an experience
of a veritable tempest of forty-eight hours' duration.   Long
afterwards it was learned from Just's companions how
cruelly he had suffered during it.   He himself, in his letters
to his parents, says nothing of this, but merely describes
the phenomena; and it is very evident that he is especially
pre-occupied with the sufferings of others.   His letters
written on ship are full of anecdotes and observations.   One
sees that he is thus endeavoring to divert his parents' attention from the to them mournful subject on which it is
concentrated—his departure.   These details written in a
simple, natural style, are very pleasant reading; and we
should reproduce them here did not frequent communication with the extreme East, at the present day, render every
one familiar with them through other sources.   What we
remark especially in Just's correspondence is the tone of
tenderness with which it is penetrated.   There was no

longer need for him to strengthen his parents in view of a coming sacrifice; the sacrifice is accomplished, and he now deems it a duty to sweeten the bitterness of their cup. It is easily seen that in doing this he follows the bent of his heart; and that, if at other times his manner seemed lacking sensibility, it was the result of violence done to himself.

Aden, Ceylon, Singapore, Saigon were the ports at which the *Cambodge* touched ere reaching Hong Kong. At Pointe de Galle (Ceylon) the missionaries landed and took a little rest. A tempest raged in the roadstead, and the debarkation was a violent gymnastic exercise, the prospect of which retained the majority of the passengers on board. But ample compensations awaited our intrepid missionaries who risked casting themselves into the ship's boat, tossed about by the rolling of the ship. Landing, they found there a Catholic mission and a church in charge of a Benedictine. Oh! what joy for them to be able to celebrate Mass, to assist even at a liturgical office, to sing and pray before the Blessed Sacrament! A few lines from Just to his parents show the fidelity with which he watched over his soul. "I longed," he writes to them, "to pray for you most especially, and *to re-animate within me the spirit of piety, somewhat weakened by the preceding bad weather, and the absence of religious exercises.*"

At Ceylon the farewells among the missionaries began, two of them going on board another ship, the destination of which was Pondicherry.

At Singapore there was a new separation, M. Groussoux leaving for Siam. After a difficult navigation, the *Cambodge* enters the Saigon river. In steaming up the river, a voice is heard from an Anamite boat going in the opposite direction. "Father Guerin," it says, "are you on board?" Our missionaries rush to the deck, just in time

to recognize two of their old confrères from Paris, whom
they had expected to find at Saigon, but whom the end of
the favorable monsoon prevented waiting there any longer.
They are now on their way to upper Cochin China. There
is an interchange of messages, letters, and especially of
fraternal tenderness. The two vessels pass on and are
soon lost to each other. At thoughts of this disappoint-
ment in Saigon, our missionaries' hearts sink within them
for an instant, but the *fiat* is soon pronounced, the apostolate is one long act of renunciation.

All their brethren, however, had not left Saigon. It is an
important mission, the seat of an Apostolic Vicariate, and
contains a church, a college, and an orphanage of the Holy
Infancy, where a hundred and twenty little Anamites receive the care of the Sisters of St. Paul de Chartres. M.
Le Méc, who was for a long time secretary to Cardinal Mar-
lot in Paris, and who after closing his archbishop's eyes in
death hastened to exchange the brilliant prospects awaiting him in France for the obscure and laborious life of the
foreign missions, is there, calm and joyous, wearing the
Anamite costume, and in a few months already familiar
with the language, and conformed to the usages of these
strange lands. Just, who had known him at the seminary,[1]
lodged now at his house, and the two enjoyed a holy and
delightful interchange of thought and feeling. But on the
missions as on campaigns, friends embrace whilst running.
That same evening the *Cambodge* gets under weigh and rede-
scends the river, for port must be gained the next day. In
the middle of the night, which was a very dark one, there
was an accident which brought out in full relief those
Christian sentiments that Just had been happy to discover
in the captain's heart. As the handsome steamer glides

---

[1] **Aspirants** (already priests) who wish to join the Society for the Foreign Missions,
have to spend at least one year at the Seminary of the Rue du Bac.

rapidly over the dark waters, cries are suddenly heard at its side, something floats and tosses in its course. It is the passengers of an Anamite junk, which, carrying no lights, has been run into by the giant that did not even feel the shock. The engineer immediately stops the machinery, but the sudden stoppage, aided by the current, carries the vessel on, and the poor Anamites are left far behind. The captain, being awakened, gives orders to send out the ship's boat to their relief. "It is useless," say all the lieutenants, "we are too far off, the night is too dark; and after all, what difference will a few Anamites less in the world make?" The captain remains firm. "I shall at least make every effort to save them. I don't wish to have their death on my conscience," he replies. Six men take their places in the ship's boat, which, guided by the distant cries of the unfortunate creatures struggling in the waters, is soon lost in the thick darkness. An hour passes, and it returns, bringing all who had been on board the Anamite junk—eight sailors, safe and sound, but greatly exhausted, having kept themselves floating on the water for nearly an hour. A missionary acquainted with their language served as interpreter; and at their request the captain had them taken in the ship's boat to a junk which one perceived at about half a league's distance. The *Cambodge* continued its course, proud that its commander was a Christian and a Frenchman. On the 28th of August, at sunrise, it entered the port of Hong Kong. The passage from Marseilles had lasted forty days.

After twenty-four hours' rest, a little American steamer took our missionaries on board, and ascending the Hong Kong River brought them to Canton, to which place our Coreans went only to accompany M. Guerrin and to visit Mgr. Guillemin, returning thence to Hong Kong.

Just's letters contain a picturesque account of these de-

barkations at Hong Kong and Canton.   The baggage intended for the missions here, and also that for Corea, must
needs be landed and taken from the wharf.   At Hong
Kong, about a hundred coolies disputed among themselves
for the transportation, and vied with one another in demanding exorbitant prices.   The missionaries were at last
obliged to resort to the only arguments these people understand—blows with a stick.   However, when one has the
heart of an apostle he does not strike very hard, and Just
and his companions took pains to hit the boxes so as to
make a great noise.   They would have remained where they
were but for the intervention of a police agent, who armed
with a long whip, which he used unsparingly, succeeded in
dispersing the band; then designating the coolies that were
to take charge of the boxes, and animating them by vigorous lashes to do their best, he ended by conducting the por-
ters and their baggage as far as the mission house.   At Canton there was the same scene on the wharf, and no officer
to come to their aid.   But experience served them instead,
and here they are at last with their loads at the house of
Mgr.. Guillemin, Vicar Apostolic of Canton.   "A poor
episcopal palace, indeed!" writes Just, "merely some hov-
els in a line, on either side of an alley, about six feet and a
half wide!. . .What a bishop and a father!   I threw myself on my knees before him, and he gave me his blessing."

Canton had been for our missionaries but the end of an
excursion; Hong Kong, to which place they soon returned,
was also only a halting-place on the journey, whence some
of them must leave for Tonquin, and the others seek means
of penetrating into Corea.   How much of the unknown still
stood between them and the region promised their apostolate!

Just and the other Coreans had intended passing only a
few days at Hong Kong.   But in the letters there awaiting

them they found new instructions. They were to stop at this port a month, to avoid remaining in Shang-Hai, which is very sickly in September; from the latter place, to which they must repair, they are to go by sea to the mouth of the Leao Ho River, and thence by land in a south-easterly direction to enter the province of Leao Tong in Mantchooria. It was here in the Vicariate Apostolic of Mgr. Verrolles they were to spend the winter, and in the spring make an attempt to penetrate into Corea.

Just writes to his parents about this new itinerary. The tone of his correspondence is changed. On board the *Cambodge* it was that of a traveller giving a humorous account of his passage. Now, having left civilization behind, it is suddenly that of the missionary in the hands of Providence, *traditus gratiæ Dei,*[1] and Faith alone will speak by his mouth. He writes: "Since it seems the will of the good God that we still wander a long time ere reaching the promised land, may it be done! Never have we been happier or more joyful than we are now. .... And do you also, dear parents, lead a life of abandonment of all things into the hands of God. We are only travellers on earth. Our country on high is very beautiful, and nothing can satisfy the thirst of the human heart, little as it is, save the endless possession of Him Who has loved us to excess. I have been told that I was foolish to think of going to Corea; but it is a folly costing one little, and most agreeable to the heart of a holy missionary, such as I wish mine were, and such as I hope it may one day be, through the grace of God." This letter now gives some details of the latter portion of his journey, and finishes thus: "Do not expect to hear from me soon. After we leave here, communication becomes more difficult. Converse with Our Lord Who loves you and Who can certainly take the place of everything

[1] Acts xx. 40.

else in your hearts. . . . Adieu, dear father and dear mother; serve God with all your strength, and beg that I too may serve Him. Pardon me all the trouble I have ever given you, likewise this verbiage which I send you, only because I believe it will give you pleasure.—Adieu, dear Christian. Where are you now and what are you doing? I know not, but I think of you very often in Our Lord. You know that there is no necessity for my writing to you: the essential thing is that we love Jesus with all the ardor of our souls. Adieu to all, and may Our Lord Jesus Christ give you His peace and His joy! "

In the last week of September the four Coreans embarked on the *Hydaspe*, a small French steamer plying between Hong Kong and Shang-Hai. Navigation was rough, and Just again experienced the sufferings incident to voyaging. On the 6th of October they took passage from Shang-Hai on the *Eclipse*, a Swedish sailing ship, for Leao Tong. Some new and rougher caprices of the ocean awaited them on this trip. Contrary winds made their descent of the Blue River and getting to sea very slow and difficult: hardly were they free of land when a violent storm came up and tossed the *Eclipse* about for two days and three nights, almost casting her on the coast of Corea. This was for our missionaries the torment of Tantalus. Thence they were driven towards China. The sea now became calm, and favorable winds took them rapidly across the Yellow Sea and the Gulf of Petchelee. When not more than forty-five miles from port, a new storm burst upon the ship, threatening to capsize it. They must needs regain the open sea again, crossing great sandy bars on which the vessel comes nigh stranding more than once; then, after being driven about for two days at the will of the hurricane, recruit at the mouth of the Leao Ho River, and cast anchor in the roadstead whilst waiting for a pilot. It was not until the 28th of October, after twenty-two days at sea, that they were at last able to land, not indeed at the river's mouth, but in a little neighboring port, *Yng-ko* or *Ing-tze.*

Behold our little band now upon the soil of Mantchooria. They carry with them a large amount of baggage, both for the mission of this country and also for that of Corea. Here the mode of travelling changes. The violence of the sea now gives place to the tediousness of a journey by land. Both men and boxes are placed in little carts without springs, each drawn by two mules harnessed tandem, that walked or trotted intrepidly, whether through marshes or down stony declivities. The carts look like wooden cages, and the jolting is so rough that in vain does the traveller hold on to the bars of his little prison; every moment he strikes against them with such force as to bruise his flesh. On arriving at the halting-place, our missionaries make acquaintance with Chinese food and the use of chop-sticks. The second halt brings them to the house of a missionary, M. Métayer, who resides at this detached station. Here, thanks to his fraternal hospitality, they at last enjoy a little rest. After passing All Saints' day with him, and satisfying the cravings of their piety, they proceed on their journey, but this time in a conveyance less painful to their limbs. On the second day they are assailed by about twenty brigands on horseback who demand the delivery of the baggage. But intimidated by the fierce attitude of the missionaries who hold their heads proudly erect, and keep their hands in their pockets because of the cold, their assailants (doubtless believing our friends were thus holding themselves in readiness to produce from those mysterious pockets some good pistols), withdrew, after escorting the caravan for an hour. At last, on the evening of this day full of excitement, our missionaries reached Notre Dame des Neiges, the residence of Mgr. Verrolles.

It had been very agreeable indeed for our poor, weary travellers to remain grouped around this holy bishop; but material necessities obliged him to disperse them. After a fortnight's relaxation here, each of the four Coreans is sent to one of the stations of the Mantchoorian mission, Just being assigned to Notre Dame du Soleil, the abode of M. Métayer, who had welcomed the caravan on its arrival in port.

Now commences for Just and his companions a new phase of their missionary life. They are to pass the winter in these cold regions, the climate of which is similar to that of Siberia, and they are to devote themselves to studying the Chinese language, scarcely less used in Corea than the native tongue, although so different.

Just's letters to his parents during this period acquaint us with his mode of life. He is nearly always at the house of M. Métayer, absorbed in the study of the Chinese letters. His active mind, ever interested in any intellectual occupation, applies itself with ardor to this trying task, the final object of which is the apostolate. In a letter to his dear friend, M. Rabardelle, missionary at Siam, he expresses the fear that he takes too much pleasure in this study. Surely he is of the race of saints to find matter herein for self-reproach. From time to time he visits Mgr. Verrolles, or some one of his brethren, scattered about over this icy region, where for five months of the year the thermometer keeps at 30° or 35° below zero. On such occasions he wears the queer costume of the country, necessitated by the rigorous climate—layers of fur garments over a sheepskin, the appearance of which is certainly curious. Accompanying the description he gave his parents of this raiment is a picture of it sketched and colored by one of his brethren. Sometimes his out-door exercise is a hunting expedition, and that he has lost none of his former skill as a marksman is evidenced by the game with which he is thus enabled to enrich the missionary's meagre table.

In mid-winter he is deprived of his companion; Mgr. Verrolles repairing to Pekin in the interests of the mission, took M. Métayer with him, and Just is thus left alone in his cold hermitage, and obliged to utilize for the ministry with which he is charged the knowledge he has already acquired of the Chinese language. What progress he had made herein his modesty leaves us to conjecture; we judge, however, that this progress was rapid, for three months after his arrival he is sufficiently advanced to give instructions to the native Christians, and to perform, with the aid of a book, the essential functions of the priesthood.

In this isolation he is happy at feeling himself entirely delivered up to Providence, destitute of all human assistance, having no companion save God,—that God Who rejoices his youth, and for Whom he has sacrificed everything. It is not in the letters he writes his parents that we must expect to find the account of his long confidences, during these winter evenings, with the divine Master. If his letters to M. Rabardelle permit us to enter more into his (Just's) spiritual life, it is to show us again with what severity he judges himself, with what zeal he humbles himself. He also knows how to give the appearance of a confession to the expression of this filial trust with which his heart is overflowing, this sure sign of true love. " I do not disquiet myself," he writes, " either as to the future or the past; I am like the horse which is guided by the bridle, and that does not seek to know whither he is driven. And if sometimes, although rarely—too rarely, perhaps—I feel a little troubled and anxious, it is only when thoughts like these present themselves: How is it that after receiving such great graces from God I still remain so spiritually weak, so sluggish, so lacking fervor in prayer, so occupied

with earth, so far from **God,** *and withal so tranquil?* **Is** not
this truly **an enigma? But** *fiat voluntas Dei.* **These
moments of fear do not last long;** for right or **wrong, I**
seek **to** dwell **rather upon the thought of the** immensity **of**
God's goodness **and love."**

The country **is infested with brigands, and** Just is obliged
to keep loaded arms in the house. Twice he **receives a**
nocturnal **visit from** these marauders. **The first time they**
act so warily that he **is not** aware of their **visit until** he dis-
covers traces **of it** the next morning. **The second time**
matters **are more serious. "** Guns **were discharged,"** he
writes, **"but I** pray you to believe it was **not I who fired."**
A **little** reflection **upon these words shows that it** was **by**
uniting intrepidity **to** the gentleness **of an** apostle, **in thus**
exposing **himself to his** assailants' fire without **returning it,**
that **he succeeded in** overcoming **them.**

Whilst preparing **to enter shortly into his dear Corea,** he
takes **an active interest in** other **missions; in the mission of**
Mantchooria, **of** which **he is the** guest, and **which offers so**
little consolation **to Mgr. Verrolles' patient zeal and perse-**
verance; **in those of Thibet and of Tonquin, already** watered
with so much blood, and **now tried by** the severest contradictions, **news of** which, reaching **him by the** messengers he
receives, **moves** him **to** give **vent to** his **feelings** thus **in a**
letter **to** M. Albrand: **" It is very** hard **for the missions**
but **very** consoling **for the** missionaries, as it **gives them a**
glimmering **hope of** martyrdom. When I think **of this I**
am on the **point of** complaining **to** Our **Lord for not** calling
me **to** receive **so great a grace. I am, indeed, far from**
being worthy of it. **But have there not been martyrs who**
were once great **sinners ? "**

The most recent news **from** Corea announced **a revolution**
favorable to Christianity, **or,** at least, **giving hope of** tolera-
tion; and Just, **on** the eve **of** going thither, **regarded with**

an eye of holy envy those of his brethren whom he believed more exposed than he would be. And yet, at that very time, none was nearer the crown than himself.

We borrow from this same letter to the Superior of the Foreign Missions a final quotation which helps depict the perfect detachment to which our young apostle had arrived ere entering the lists. " Permit me to remind you," it says, " that on leaving Paris I placed entirely at your disposal the money which at times would be remitted you for me. If then some of my brethren, *or even of other missions*, can put it to a better use than I, send it to them. I leave the disposition of it entirely to your judgment."

Winter was at an end; and the breaking up of the ice opened the rivers and harbors. The time had now come when our Coreans must make an attempt to enter the country. Access to Corea was at this time so difficult to Europeans, less because of hatred of the Christian name than the Corean government's mistrust of all foreigners, even the Chinese, and the Draconian laws forbidding the natives to trade with outsiders. Our missionaries must needs embark on a Chinese junk, and go to find at some point on the Corean coast a Corean vessel. The appointment for one had been made nearly a year previously, but a thousand events might occur in the meantime to frustrate the meeting; in that case a new attempt was to be made at the end of July, and if it failed, all further efforts to penetrate into the country must be abandoned until the following spring. Moreover, the meeting must take place secretly, in a secluded spot. Were it discovered, baggage and missionaries —all would be lost. This very year two Corean barks carrying no Europeans whatever, being suspected of communication with China, were seized in the Seoul river, and all on board beheaded without even a trial.

Just now touches upon the most solemn hour of his life.

By the aid of address and courage, resolution and patience, he was going to force a passage which would introduce him either into a long career in the apostolate or to the short, straight road of martyrdom. This explains the firm, unwavering tone of his correspondence. When the chords of the will are attuned to heroism, their notes are strong and resonant. He would also see those he loves raised like himself above the most allowable weaknesses of the heart. On the 2d of April he writes thus to his parents: "If the good God favor our attempt to enter Corea, this letter will be the last you may expect to receive from me for a year. I regret your having to suffer this little privation. In one sense, however, I do not regret it, for it is a privation carrying with it the grace of God. The road leading to heaven is all sown with thorns, and the more our feet are torn by them the better for us will it be. Let us beg God to make us comprehend that one hour of suffering here is far more precious than a whole year of delights. We never dream of complaining; on the contrary, in the joy of our hearts, we render thanks to God for the blessings he showers upon us every moment."

On the 24th of April Just left his residence at Notre Dame du Soleil in company with M. Dorie, who had come here to join him, the two taking M. Beaulieu to his winter station, distant about a day's journey. There they found M. Huin. On the 26th of the same month all four reached Notre Dame des Neiges, to make their final preparations.

May 1st, putting themselves under the Blessed Virgin's protection, they started for the port of Tsouang Ho, and next day they engaged passage in a little junk, manned by Chinese infidels, but good, reliable men. The sea being too rough to set sail immediately, they did not leave port until May 3d. A strong wind from the north bore them rapidly before it to the shores of Corea, and on the morning of the

5th land was in sight. Suddenly the wind changed, bearing directly down upon them, and they were forced to seek shelter under the lea of a little island called Kio Tao, fifteen leagues to the north of Melinto. The state of the sea kept them for eight days in this cove, in constant dread lest the violence of the waters break their moorings and dash them upon the rocks. Meanwhile their provisions gave out, the supply having been laid in for a much shorter voyage, and the hostile disposition of the islanders did not permit them to land and replenish. One night especially the tempest was terrible; the junk was nigh foundering at the anchorage. The sufferings of all on board were indescribable. Notwithstanding the peril from wind and wave, they must make an attempt to keep their appointment with the Corean vessel, and themselves constrained by the necessity of it, the missionaries forced the Chinese to put to sea again; but very soon the latter lose courage, and it is the priests who take charge of the vessel. One whole day's navigation in the face of a contrary wind, amid a thousand dangers, entailing upon our intrepid voyagers extreme fatigue, was futile, and they were delighted in the evening to regain the shelter they had left at morn. Next day the sea is still rough, but the wind is changed. Again the missionaries constrain their men to put to sea in a pouring rain. The former take turns at the watch, guiding the vessel through a thick mist by means of little compasses which Just's parents had given each one at the moment of departure. Towards noon the mist clears away, and reveals to them at a distance of about three miles a formidable cape which they must double. At the point of this cape there is a dread whirlpool, similar, it is said, to the Maelstrom on the Norway coast. Boldly entering this perilous region, our travellers, who have had no inconsiderable experience of great storms at sea, now believe that they have indeed encountered the

fury of the elements for the first time. The wind rent the
junk's sails and broke a mast; huge waves dashed over the
vessel and threatened to engulf it. Had it not been sea-
worthy, strong, and all the seams tightly caulked, it would
certainly have gone down in an instant. Terrified, the
Chinese prostrated themselves before their idols. The missionaries made a vow to Mary, Star of the sea. At last
the cape is doubled, and on the evening of this same day the
vessel casts anchor at Melinto.

But now a new trial awaits them: the Corean bark which
was to meet them is not here. It had been seized and con-
fiscated by the mandarins. Mgr. Berneux, Vicar Apostolic
of Corea, learned this at the last moment, and immediately
set about finding another. He succeeded, but the substi-
tute was in such a condition that he deemed it a duty to
tell the Christians who were to man it that they were free
to attempt or to abandon the undertaking. Happily these
good men decided upon the former, and reached Melinto
on the night of the 18th or 19th of May. "Towards eleven
o'clock at night," writes Just, "the sea being calm and
smooth as a mirror, hearing a bark quietly approaching us,
and the name of our bishop pronounced by those on board,
we recognize the arrival of the brave Christians who exposed
their necks to the sabre to come for us."

For six days had the missionaries been foiled in their attempts. Only twenty-four hours more and the expiration
of the appointed time, as well as want of provisions, would
have constrained them to return anew to Leao Tong.

Sixteen days they had been on the water, either sailing
or stationary, almost without food, reduced to a few hand-
fuls of rice. The violence of the sea had brought them
two or three fowls, which had been long since consumed.

The transfer of the baggage was soon made. Two hastily-
written notes, one to Mgr. Verrolles in Mantchooria, and

one to M. Albrand in Paris, announcing the successful issue
of the voyage, were confided to the Chinese sailors; and
towards midnight the missionaries passed over to the
Corean bark. They were not yet at the end of their
trials.

Sixty leagues separated them from the spot at which
they were to land. Contrary winds and the dangerous
currents circulating between the numberless islands which
surround Corea rendered navigation difficult and slow.
After five days' efforts they reached the designated landing,
but the Christians guiding them having learned the rigorous
fate, only a few days before, of the crew of two barks suspected by the mandarin of communication with the Chinese,
deemed it more prudent, instead of going up the river, to slip
quietly along the shore, and debark forty leagues farther
southward. At last, on the 27th of May, after four days
more of sailing, our poor, weary travellers set foot upon
the soil of their new country. Whilst repairing to a
Christian settlement, they chanted in their hearts a *Te
Deum* of thanksgiving.

"Everybody in Corea," writes Just, "pagan as well as
Christian, knew that four new missionaries were to arrive
shortly." However, they were not expected to come here.
It was a joyful surprise, and the welcome these poor people
gave them was eager and cordial. Mgr. Daveluy, coadjutor to the Vicar Apostolic, resided about two leagues distant.
He hastened next morning to receive the missionaries, and
without loss of time dispatched Just to the Vicar Apostolic,
Mgr. Berneux, whilst he himself embarked that night with
MM. Dorie, Beaulieu, and Huin, to conduct them to a more
isolated Christian settlement.

Just, soon clothed in the Corean costume, wearing straw
sandals too short for his feet, started out for a four days'
walk across the mountains, going to surprise the holy Bish-

op, who had begun to despair. His confrères followed him a few days later.

The period of preparation for the novices of the apostolate had ended. From Marseilles to Sèoul, from the 19th of July, 1864, to May 27, 1865, more than ten months, they had endured all the annoyances and hardships of travelling, together with the anxiety of the expectation, delay, and hope deferred. They now entered upon a new phase of labors and sufferings, in this field which the missionary waters always with his sweat and his tears, and often with his blood.

CHAPTER V.

ABRIDGED SKETCH OF THE COREAN MISSION UP TO THE ARRIVAL OF JUST AND HIS COMPANIONS (1781–1865).

THE portion of the world into which our four young missionaries had just penetrated was at that time but slightly known to Europeans. Nevertheless, Christianity had already a history there—a heroic history, the outlines of which we lay before our readers, space not permitting us to dwell longer upon it. Mgr. Daveluy, who set foot on Corean soil in 1845, had succeeded, during these twenty years, amid all the overwhelming labors of his ministry, in collecting on the spot everything relative to the establishment, origin, and growth of Christianity here, as well as many interesting souvenirs of its trials and vicissitudes. It was from these notes, which he sent to France a year before his martyrdom, that the historical work [1]

---

[1] *Histoire de l'Église de Corée* (History of the Church in Corea), by Ch. Dallet, priest of the Society of Foreign Missions.—Paris, Palmé, 1874,

from which we borrow our information was compiled.

Corea is a large, mountainous peninsula, flanked upon the west by an elongated archipelago. It forms a tract the greatest width of which is about one hundred and thirty leagues, and which, although slightly deflected, extends almost regularly from north to south three hundred leagues, parallel to the western coast of China. Italy, were it extended less towards the south-east, and were Naples its southern extremity, would be a sufficiently correct representation of the shape of this territory. A vassal of China, to which it annually sends an embassy with presents, Corea nevertheless forms an autonomous kingdom, the idiom and usages of which differ materially from those of the former country. The Corean government, up to the period at which our narration begins, had, even more jealously than the Chinese, guarded its security in an absolute isolation. The events of 1860 which opened China to European commerce could have thrown down these barriers. But the heads of the Anglo-French expedition, strangers to all that concerned Corea, were even ignorant of the panic which their victory caused here. At that time the appearance of a frigate along the shores of the peninsula, only forty leagues from Shang-Hai, had been all sufficient to open to civilization and liberty this inhospitable land. The two squadrons left the China Sea without even suspecting what a glorious opportunity they had let slip; and six years afterwards the Catholic missionaries were still the only Europeans who had succeeded in clearing this rampart of barbarism—and this at the risk of their lives, employing a thousand artifices to accomplish their purpose.

And yet this land, thus separated from the entire world by secular prejudices, is inhabited by an amiable, gentle people, better disposed, perhaps, than any other to receive the good seed of the Gospel. Whilst elsewhere Christianity advances with slow steps, religious liberty even not sufficing to accelerate its progress, the conversion of adults being rare, and the Church owing its increase to the work of the Holy Infancy and the orphanages, here the moral superiority of the Christian doctrine is enough of itself to gain partisans among persons who hear it spoken of for the first time.

In this respect the evangelization of Corea presents a phenomenon unique, we believe, in the history of modern missions. We must go back to the primitive evangelization to find its counterpart.

We justly admire the constancy of the faithful Japanese, who, surviving the frightful persecutions of two centuries ago, guarded and transmitted to their descendants the essential elements of religion, thus keeping alive two hundred years a latent Christianity, without priests, without a hierarchy, without any sacrament except baptism, without any apostolate save that of the family, until a very recent day, when Japan, opening in turn her gates to the world, brought our missionaries into the presence of these glorious heirs of a Faith which their persecutors thought had been stifled in blood.

Beyond doubt, it was an admirable example of supernatural vitality. Japan, however, had received the Gospel from the hands of St. Francis Xavier, and for a century Christianity had flourished there. When it disappeared from the kingdom, drowned in waves of blood, the survivors of so many massacres bore with them to their retreat the souvenirs of a religious life, lacking none of those resources which the Church, when in full possession of her freedom, showers upon her children.

Corea, however, presents to us a spectacle altogether different. It was a country cut off from the outer world and it had never seen a priest. About the end of the eigh-

teenth century several of its sages, who applied themselves
to the research for moral truth, fell upon some religious
treatises written in Chinese and imported into China,
apparently by accident, with a lot of scientific works. In
1783 one of these sages, Peter Seng-Houn-i, who was
one of the embassy that Corea sends annually to Pekin,
becoming acquainted with the Bishop of that city, the illustrious Alexander Govea, a Portuguese Franciscan, was
converted and baptized. Returning to his own country
he took with him religious books, crucifixes and pictures,
which he distributed among his acquaintances. Aided by
his friend, the virtuous Piek-i, and other imitators of his zeal,
he began to disseminate a knowledge of the Faith, address-
ing himself in preference to the most enlightened and
learned men—men renowned for their wisdom. The fervent catechists even accepted public discussions with the
followers of Fo and Lao Tse, who were very numerous in
Corea. These philosophical tilts turned to the honor of
the Christian religion, which thus obtained at the outset an
honorable notoriety in the world of letters, whence it was
diffused among the middle and lower classes of the population. The catechumens baptized by Seng-Houn-i baptized others in turn. They translated into Corean the
books composed by the Chinese missionaries; they initiated
the neophytes into Christian practices—the sanctification
of Sunday, the observance of fasts and abstinences, even
the rigors of asceticism; they inculcated, according to the
measure of their lights on the subject, the Christian discipline of marriage; in a word, they established, with the
inevitable gaps consequent upon such a condition of affairs,
a society of the faithful, attached to the Church in
China by baptism—all this brought about by the voluntary apostolate of one convert who ever remained a
layman.

Such a commencement was of itself a prodigy.   The sequel is still more surprising.

The infant Church of Corea had to wait ten years for the arrival of the first Catholic priest who penetrated into the kingdom.

Unceasingly did the Christians of this country entreat the Bishop of Pekin to send them evangelical laborers; but obstacles innumerable prevented his complying with their request.   Meanwhile privation of spiritual aid was so sensibly felt by them that in their ignorance of the laws of the sacred hierarchy, believing that they could transmit the priesthood even as they could confer baptism, they ordained a bishop and several priests, imitating therein the ceremonies which Peter Seng-Houn-i had witnessed in Pekin, and making for the celebration of the holy mysteries suitable altar vessels and precious ornaments.   Informed of their error by the Bishop of Pekin, the pseudo priests renounced their usurped ministry with touching humility, and renewed their entreaties to obtain priests from China.   But ere receiving so great a grace the young Corean Church must needs render to Jesus Christ her first testimony of blood.

The imperfection of their theological knowledge, which had permitted the heads of this Christian community to take upon themselves the priesthood, left them equally ignorant of their duty regarding the ceremonies in honor of ancestors.   These rites practised in China had, after celebrated controversies, been condemned by the Holy See as tainted with idolatrous superstition.   They were scarcely different in Corea, and the people's attachment to them not less than it was in China.   A characteristic of the Coreans is filial piety, and these funeral rites are the principal expression of it.

When instructions on this point arrived from Pekin, the Corean Christians had no alternative but to renounce either these rites or the Faith. Only a very small number accepted the latter alternative. The rest submitted, but the propagation of the Gospel was arrested; the profession of Christianity assumed in the eyes of the pagans an appearance of impiety; and all the abhorrence that the new religion had already aroused, the prejudices formed against it in the old Corean party, an enemy to any communication with the stranger, now found a plausible pretext for the employment of the most merciless measures for stamping it out. A first persecution burst forth in 1791; and the constancy of the neophytes amid tortures was wonderful. Alas! there were also apostates; some who had endured tortures permitting themselves to be overcome by the entreaties of their relatives, or the fear of involving these in a common ruin. And even among those who had been the first propagators of the Gospel were some deplorable instances of falling away from the Faith. But others gloriously repaired the weakness of these, and died martyrs in the persecutions which followed. Numberless were the heroes who stood firm amid the horrible experience of dislocations of the joints, cudgeling of the limbs, and the rack. The persecutors' cruelty only furnished these heroes the opportunity of spreading the tidings of salvation. The interrogatories, always accompanied with tortures, attracted numberless spectators, before whom the confessors of the Faith, unjustly accused of impiety or of immorality, unfolded in long discourses the various articles of Christian belief, thus displaying to the eyes of all the radiant beauty of the Gospel, and forcing words of admiration for its excellence even from the judges themselves. More than one conversion dates its origin from these sublime instructions delivered on the rack.

It was thus the Corean Church prepared itself in tears and blood to receive God's messenger, who came at last, in

the person of Father James Tsiou, a Chinese priest, sent
hither by the Bishop of Pekin in 1794, just ten years after
the baptism of the first Corean convert.   He found on his
arrival more than four thousand Christians in Corea, and
the peaceful virtues of virginity, humility, mortification,
charity flourishing in this new-born scion of Christendom
beside the palms its first martyrs had so gloriously won.

The ministry of Father Tsiou exercised amidst continual
alarms was as fruitful as it was laborious.   The general
persecutions had ceased, but liberty was not restored to
the Church, and she was kept under pressure by local annoyances and the malevolent designs of individuals.   The
king was opposed to violent measures, but the cruelty, or
the cupidity, of the mandarins still made martyrs here and
there.

Five years of peace, broken in upon by bloody episodes,
passed away; and during this time Christianity made
rapid progress.   But the death of the king in 1799 and
the establishment of a regency gave full sway to the tyranny of ministers and mandarins; and after most cruel pre-
liminaries, an edict of the regent inaugurated, in 1801,
the second general persecution, which was long and terrible.   The avowed intention of the Corean government was
to exterminate the dangerous sect of Christians.   Father
Tsiou, perceiving that the hatred of the pagans was directed
especially against strangers, thought to ameliorate the fate
of his followers by delivering himself up to his persecutors.
After undergoing the usual tortures, he was beheaded on
the 31st of May, 1801.

This generous sacrifice did not disarm the fury of the
enemies of Christianity.   The number of victims in the
provinces was never exactly ascertained.   In the capital
alone it exceeded three hundred, both sexes, every condition of life, every age furnishing their contingent to the

army of martyrs; and the annals of the Corean Church are enriched with souvenirs comparable to those of Lawrence and Agnes in the Church at Rome.

The persecution, ofttimes fatigued by its own fury, would pause at intervals, but only to reanimate itself; and it may be said that really from the beginning of the century until very recently never entirely ceased. Scarcely a year passed that did not see there Christians imprisoned for their faith, interrogated, tortured, put to death or exiled when not forgotten in their horrible prisons, and left to die of hunger amid sufferings unutterable.

Let us here call attention to the following facts: founded in 1784 by the voluntary apostolate of Peter Seng-Houn-i, this unparalleled branch of Christendom had to wait until 1831 for the establishment of a Vicariate Apostolic, and until 1836 for the entrance into Corea of the first European missionary, M. Maubant. During these fifty-two years it had no exterior succor save the ministry of Father Tsiou, which was of five years' duration. For forty-seven years it sustained itself without priests, with no sacrament but baptism, with no preaching but that of catechists; it passed through the general persecutions of 1791, 1801, 1815, 1827; and it furnished the Church more than a thousand martyrs, innumerable confessors of the Faith, and multiplied examples of the most admirable virtues.

Time and again these poor, isolated Corean Christians would send touching addresses to the Sovereign Pontiff, supplicating him to grant them apostolic laborers. Pius VII. received their homage in 1792, at the beginning of the French Revolution, and placed them under the jurisdiction of the Bishop of Pekin. But soon the Church in China itself felt the effects of that terrible storm which swept over Europe, and the hopes of Corea were swallowed

up in the confusion.   In 1811 Pius VII. received another
letter from the faithful Coreans; but this time their
petition found him a prisoner at Fontainebleau.   When the
events of 1815 restored peace to the world, the Church and
Europe had many cruel wounds to heal.   There were gaps
to be filled up in the ranks of the priesthood, the wants of
the religious orders which had been suppressed or dispersed to be supplied, and whilst thus providing for the
necessities of worship and of the apostolate in our own
country, new laborers were to be recruited for the foreign
missions.

Whilst the Seminary of the Foreign Missions, re-estab-
lished, then closed anew by Napoleon in 1809, had again
just re-opened in Paris, and the Sacred Congregation of
the Propaganda was endeavoring to provide, out of its scanty
resources, for the necessities of Christians deprived of
spiritual aid, another appeal from the Coreans reached
Rome, now under the Pontificate of Leo XII.   Written in
1825, it did not reach the Pope until 1827, just at the
time when a new general persecution was ravaging the
Church in Corea.

Touched by such unwavering and persistent fidelity, the
Sovereign Pontiff charged the Propaganda to offer the
Corean mission to the Society of the Foreign Missions.
Having consulted all its members, even the most distant,
the Society accepts, despite the insufficiency of its resources both of men and money, and permits one of its
priests, M. Bruguière, to offer himself for the inaugura-
tion of this perilous ministry.

This courageous missionary had just arrived in Siam to
assist the venerable Mgr. Florent, Vicar Apostolic of that
country, who, weighed down by toil and years, had applied
for a coadjutor.   Rivaling each other in generosity, the
Bishop and priest both consented, the one to deprive him-

self of much needed assistance, the other to exchange a peaceful and pleasant service for an unknown mission, bristling with difficulties and perils. Consecrated Bishop in 1829, Mgr. Bruguière was nominated Vicar Apostlic of Corea by Gregory XVI. in 1834.

But the trials of the poor Corean Christians, so long without a pastor, were not yet over.

More closed than ever against strangers, and especially Christians, Corea could not be entered except by stealth. To penetrate into the country, the new Vicar Apostolic undertook a journey which lasted three years, during which time he made acquaintance both on land and at sea with all the sufferings, all the perils that St. Paul enumerates when giving the account of his own apostolate. Meanwhile, a Chinese priest, Father Pacificus, had gained entrance into Corea and commenced to administer the sacraments; but far from facilitating the exercise of the authority of the Vicar Apostolic, he thought only of opposing it, filling the hearts of the Coreans with terror, telling them that the arrival of the French Bishop would only enkindle the stifled fires of persecution. More a Chinese than a priest, this unworthy missionary thus combated the work of God. Such infidelity caused him to lose the grace of his vocation; and whilst listening to the voice of ambition, by striving to render himself necessary, and acting with the authority of a bishop, he fell into the snares of the tempter, and disgraced himself by secret disorders, which, discovered later, forced the head of the mission, M. Maubant, to send him away.

Mgr. Bruguière had much to suffer from the silent hostility of his spiritual children even whilst making strenuous efforts to appear among them,—a hostility due the influence of Father Pacificus. They were continually raising up new difficulties to delay his entrance among them

—imaginary difficulties invented for that express purpose.
At last it became necessary for the intrepid Bishop to resort to severity, and threaten the Coreans with the excom-
munication pronounced against those who embarrassed
the ministry of the Holy See's envoys.   The simple, humble faith of these good people could not resist longer; and
everything was put in readiness to welcome Mgr. Bruguï-
ère.   But just when about to attain the object of his generous desires, the holy Bishop, whose energies had been ex-
pended in a superhuman struggle, succumbed suddenly to
nervous prostration, and died at Sivang, in Western Tartary,
on the 20th of October, 1835.   Leaving Singapore on the
12th of September, 1832, from that time until the hour of
his death he had been engaged in one incessant struggle
against the innumerable obstacles which interposed themselves between him and the land of his adoption.

Whilst the Church in Corea thus became widowed by
the death of her first pastor, whom she had never even seen,
a French missionary, M. Maubant, who had been appointed
to assist Mgr. Bruguière, succeeded in entering Corea.
Another French priest, M. Chaston, followed close upon his
footsteps.   For five years these two missionaries labored
alone in this field watered with the blood of so many martyrs.   They found about nine thousand Christians in Corea,
and the zeal of our two missionaries notably increased the
number.   Religion now made great progress indeed in this
isolated land.   They also organized the Church here, which
had never known the blessings of spiritual government, and
they utilized to its full extent this period of comparative
peace which God accorded them.

At the end of the year 1837 a new Vicar Apostolic, Mgr.
Imbert, succeeded in penetrating into the kingdom.   It
seemed as if brighter days were now about to dawn upon
this sorely tried portion of God's vineyard.   A Bishop and

two priests—more than it had ever seen on its soil at once since its foundation. But, alas! two years more and a furious persecution burst forth. The three missionaries, imitating Father Tsiou's devotedness, endeavored to avert its fury from their flock by sacrificing themselves. The Bishop, delivering himself up first, sent word to his two companions to join him. On the 21st of September, 1839, all three consummated, by decapitation, their confession of the Faith—a confession begun amid tortures.

The persecution of 1839 was more general and more methodical than any that had preceded it. The martyrs were numberless, and apostasies rare, especially in the capital. Even those who, overcome by torture, apostatized with their lips, still kept alive in the depths of their hearts the germ of faith, which led them to repentance.

The Corean Church was again without pastors, and more than five years passed ere it saw another minister of Christ. During this time, intermittent periods of persecution again enriched its martyrology, notably in 1841, a year celebrated in its annals for the heroism of its confessors of the Faith. M. Ferréol, who had sought to join Mgr. Imbert in Corea at the time of the latter's martyrdom, had been appointed to succeed him; but he had not yet been able to force the rigorous blockade established all along the Corean frontier to prevent the entrance of Europeans. Consecrated Bishop in Mantchooria by Mgr. Verrolles in 1843, he finally succeeded in entering the country by sea, in company with M. Daveluy, and a young Corean priest named Andrew Kim. The latter had been ordained in China, and his intrepid constancy, during three years of incredible trials and labors, had prepared the way for the success of his efforts. Later on, when before the judges who interrogated him, the narration of his adventures excited a cry of admiration even from his persecutors. " Poor young man," they exclaimed on hearing his history, " in what terrible labors has he not consumed his youth!"

Mgr. Ferréol found his Church desolated, the Christians dispersed, disheartened, and, humanly speaking, ruined. Everything had to be commenced anew; discipline was relaxed, instruction neglected, and even a portion of his flock had concealed themselves from him in terror. Whilst he, assisted by M. Daveluy, lay hold of this great undertaking, Andrew Kim, sent on ahead of the two missionaries, fell into the hands of the official satellites, and, after a heroic confession of the Faith, shed his blood for Jesus Christ with celestial joy, September 16, 1846. This was the signal for new arrests, and the year 1846 again saw Christian martyrs in Corea.

Our task would be incomplete unless we gave here some account, even though much abridged, of the vicissitudes and trials through which the Church in Corea continued to pass. Whilst the two French missionaries were vainly endeavoring to cross the frontiers, M. Ferréol occupied himself in setting in order the affairs of his episcopal charge. A Corean deacon, Thomas T'soi, sent to China to study for the ministry, succeeded in re-entering Corea, where soon after he was ordained. A French missionary, M. Maistre, after several fruitless attempts. finally forced his way into the country, but he arrived only to see his Bishop die, worn out by fatigues and privations. This made the third Vicar Apostolic that the Church had lost in Corea within ten years.

The Holy See appointed a worthy successor in the person of Mgr. Berneux, who had confessed the Faith amid torture in the persecution in Tonquin. Condemned to death, he escaped his fate only by the timely arrival of a French frigate which demanded the prisoner's release. God still reserved for the holy Bishop the palm of martyrdom, but

He desired him to gain it by ten more years of hardships.

Two other missionaries, MM. Pourthié and Petit-Nicolas, also penetrated into Corea with M. Berneux, setting foot upon the soil at Easter, in the year 1856. All three were destined to receive the crown of martyrdom.

Already enfeebled by work and suffering, the new Vicar Apostolic had not accepted the perilous charge offered him except to renew the episcopate in the bosom of his Church. Scarcely acquainted with the state of his clergy, he hastened to avail himself of the powers received from Rome to select a coadjutor. There could be no doubt as to his choice. An incomparable missionary, initiated ten years previously into the Corean language and manners, M. Daveluy was the soul of the mission, and Mgr. Berneux gave him episcopal consecration March 25, 1857.

Just about the time of this happy event a new evangelical laborer, M. Féron, came to join Mgr. Berneux, who could thus hold a synod composed of two bishops, four French and one Corean priest. It really seemed again as if brighter days were in store for this sorely tried Church.

A sad loss soon tempered Mgr. Berneux's joy. M. Maistre succumbed to a short illness almost immediately after the arrival of M. Féron. The holy Bishop did not give way to discouragement, but bravely set about the administration of the affairs of his diocese, fully resolved to resign the pastoral staff in a very short time to M. Daveluy. But the needs of the mission did not permit him to carry out his design. Although sick and emaciated, he could not limit himself to the mere management, he must take an active part. The Gospel made rapid progress, favored by a lull in the storms of persecution, thus giving the Christians a little respite. It was absolutely necessary that he assume the administration of a vast district.

Each missionary had his own territory over which he

must travel during the winter months, going from village to village, and always taking the strictest precautions to pass through unobserved. The two Bishops conducted themselves like simple priests, walking a part of the day through snow and ice, and spending the remainder of it in receiving the visits of the faithful, in examining into their affairs, recording the marriages, instructing and baptizing catechumens and hearing confessions. A few hours' sleep on a straw mat was all the repose they could allow themselves. They must arise at midnight, hear confessions again, say Mass, give Communion to the faithful assembled from all the neighboring localities, and leave before daybreak, so as to avoid attracting the attention of the pagans. Mgr. Berneux, seeing all the heroism required of his missionaries, had determined to set them the example. Always up at half-past two in the morning, he continued laboring or walking until evening; and then not until an advanced hour did he cease work, to throw himself almost worn out upon his mat. Add to all this the insufficiency of food in a poor country in which the greater part of the inhabitants live habitually on rice and herbs, the missionary receiving hospitality of the Christians only, who are nearly always ruined materially by persecutions, and you will have some idea of the superhuman existence which is the ordinary condition of the apostolate in this country. " I have always led a life of sobriety and labor," wrote the Bishop of Capse, " but I really think that now I have reached the *ne plus ultra.* "

Mgr. Daveluy, imitating the virtues of the Vicar Apostolic, administered like him the affairs of a district; and in summer, during which time the Christians are absorbed in their field labors, he occupied his leisure in compiling a large Chinese-Corean and French dictionary, in writing in Corean books on religion, and in collecting from the lips of the aged souvenirs of the implanting of the Faith and of the persecutions of Christians in Corea.

So great zeal could not but be fruitful. For the year 1859 there were registered 607 baptisms of adults, over 1700 baptisms of infants, 908 of which were those of pagan infants at the point of death, over 1200 catechumens, nearly 1400 confessions and over 7000 communions, over 200 Christian marriages, etc. The Christian population exceeded 16,000.

The Christian religion was now beginning to prosper in Corea, when at the commencement of the year 1860 the hatred and cupidity of a mandarin, judge of a criminal court and head of the police in the capital, suddenly aroused the slumbering fires of a partial persecution, which cast terror into the faithful. The king and the government were not favorable to rigorous measures; hence the mandarin's malevolent zeal was disavowed, and the Christians who had been arrested and interrogated were not executed; but numerous acts of violence were committed, the houses of the faithful being delivered over to pillage by his satellites, whole villages burnt or razed to the ground, and their unhappy inhabitants obliged to flee to the mountains in the direst distress. This storm of persecution made havoc with the Christians, and for a time arrested the progress of evangelization.

A calm had hardly ensued ere the news reached Corea of the result of the Anglo-French expedition to Pekin. Terror spread throughout the country. Those who were at the head of the government were almost wild, expecting. from day to day, to behold a European fleet upon their coasts. By degrees the panic gave way to a feeling of contempt for *the barbarians of the West.* Nothing could have been more unfortunate for the mission, as the events of 1866 abundantly prove.

It was just at this troubled period that Mgr. Berneux had to deplore the death of Father Thomas T'soi, the young Corean priest, a worthy rival of the virtues of his French brethren, and doubly precious to the mission by reason of his nationality. This loss was repaired in part by the arrival of four new missionaries, MM. Landre, Joanno, Calais, and Ridel. The first two scarcely did more than appear in Corea, for in the course of the year 1863 they were both carried off by sickness. In June of the same year a fifth priest sent from France, M. Aumaitre, after an unsuccessful attempt in the spring, now succeeded in penetrating into Corea, and came as a balm of consolation to the heart of the Vicar Apostolic, steeped in sorrow and consumed by cares.

It was necessarily several months before the newly-arrived missionaries could be of any service to the missions. "I put them out in Christian houses," said Mgr. Berneux. There, separated from all intercourse with their compatriots, they learned the language more rapidly, and received, from time to time, the consoling visit of the holy Bishop, who taught them even more by example than word the apostolic art of finding joy amid work and suffering.

Thus, assisted by a coadjutor and eight priests, Mgr. Berneux could now promise himself some blessed fruits of his zeal; but a revolution in the palace annihilated his hopes. The king died at the beginning of the year 1864. Although worthless and enfeebled by·debauchery, he had at least a mild disposition, and was an enemy to all rigorous measures. Weak character as he was, his influence over state affairs had helped to stifle, in its germ, the persecution of 1860; and his death gave the reins anew into the hands of the persecutors. One of the four crowned widows, Queen Tého, stealthily obtaining possession of the royal seal, transmitted the throne, in the name of the dead king, according to the

Corean custom, to a prince of her choice. He was a child but twelve years old; hence by this means she assured herself of the regency.

To accomplish this stroke of audacity, she had to make use of a faction composed of the worst enemies of Christianity; and although personally not given to violent measures, she had to select her ministers from among the partisans of persecution. Thus were brought about the terrible events which, two years later, were almost to annihilate Christianity in Corea.

The first symptoms of this change of politics were felt in the provinces. The central government gave no signal for these troubles, but the mandarins now saw themselves more at liberty to gratify their hatred and cruelty. From the end of the year 1865 the provinces of Hoang Hai and Pieng-an were the theatre of violence, arbitrary arrests, tortures or sentences of banishment decreed against Christians. Lawlessness went still farther in Kieng-Sang, and ended in the martyrdom of two heroic young men, who, after confessing the Faith amid frightful tortures, were finally strangled in prison.

The storm did not reach the interior; and Mgr. Berneux, more and more worn out by fatigues and infirmities, could resume the apostolic work with the aid of new assistants. The letters of Mgr. Daveluy, in 1865, note most admirable traits of fidelity and virtue among mere catechumens, showing what extraordinary preparation of heart these poor Coreans brought to the evangelical culture.

The diseases which succeeded in ruining the health of the elder missionaries, and made great inroads upon that of all new-comers, were the only notable trails that the mission passed through up to the time when Just and his companions reached the end of the perilous journey, the vicissitudes of which we have already related.

We must now resume our biographical sketch.   Without
losing sight for an instant of our hero, we shall see unfolding before our eyes that bloody drama which of a Christian
mission already beginning to flourish left nothing but ruins.

CHAPTER VI.

LIFE IN COREA.—THE MARTYRDOM (1865–1866).

W E left our four missionaries with Mgr. Daveluy, who
had received them on their arrival.   Just was sent
thence to Mgr. Berneux at Séoul, the capital of the kingdom,
two of his confrères joining him there a few days later.   M.
Huin remained with Mgr. Daveluy.   Having made the acquaintance of his new co-laborers, the Bishop of Capse now
assigned MM. Beaulieu and Dorie a residence in the province, and retained M. de Bretenières at Séoul.

However, he did not wish to keep him in what Just
humorously styled the episcopal hut; but to facilitate the
latter's acquirement of the language of the country he
placed him in a house of native Christians, whence the
young missionary, from time to time, went to visit him at
night, to enkindle his zeal at the home of this true apostle.

Just's correspondence furnishes us with some interesting
details concerning the new mode of living which he must
now adopt.   Corea, as we have already stated, is a poor
country, and it was then entirely closed to commerce.   One
finds there scarcely any artisans, strictly speaking.   Each one
cultivates his field and provides by his own industry for the
various necessities of life, constructing his house, making
his clothing, his shoes, and even the instruments his work

requires.   Hence from great inexperience results great imperfection in the products of their labor.

"Behold me now become a citizen of the capital," writes
Just to his old preceptor, "and this is saying not a little,
for the name of our city signifies *city of delights*.   But do
not allow yourself to be dazzled by this magnificent name.
Everything is relative in this world, and what might be delightful to a Corean would be far from such to a European.
Figure to yourself an immense agglomeration of huts, built
of earth and scarcely comparable in appearance to the poor-
est huts of Bresse, all crowded close together, having between them, in place of streets, only narrow passages in
which two persons could scarcely pass.   These alleys also
serve for drains, and are always flowing with filth of every
sort without exception.   You can imagine what it must be
to splash through them, especially in rainy weather."

The interior of these huts is not more inviting than the
exterior.   Just convinces us of this fact by the following
description of them in a letter to his parents.

"Far back in the house of the Christian," he writes, "in
a part the most retired, where, according to Corean usages,
strangers are not permitted to penetrate, is the room reserved
for the missionary—the best in the abode.   But do not
believe it is anything very grand—far from it indeed, the
dimensions of the room being about five feet in height, ten
in length, and the same in width.   One can take but three
or four steps therein in any direction.   As to furniture, that
is a matter of the future, the ground serving, according
to circumstances, as chair, bed, table, etc.   A small opening scarcely a yard high, closed by a frame covered with
paper, serves both for door and for window.   It is here the
missionary assembles around him in turn a few Christians
that they may receive the sacraments and hear Mass.   It is
also the only place that I have for exercising my long limbs

by walking. Like a squirrel in his cage, I turn and turn
again, trying to imagine myself making delightful excursions in the mountains. But oh, take care of the head!
Fortunately, the tuft of hair which stands up over the forehead like a keel continually averts the danger."

As to clothing, the attire indoors consists merely of large,
puffed-out trousers and a short jacket. When the missionary leaves the house, he adds to this a long robe made of a
sombre-colored material, resembling our wrapping cloth,
and an immense cone-shaped hat, looking like the roof of
a pigeon house, being at least half a yard high and a yard
and a half in diameter, the brim of this strange head-gear
reaching to the elbows. This is the mourning costume of
the Coreans; and the missionaries adopted it because in
that country any one who has lost his parents being
obliged to cover his face, it thus afforded them (the missionaries) an excellent mode of concealing their European
features from curious observers.

The food is not more enviable, and worse than all, it is
insufficient in nourishment, the missionary's strength soon
failing on this diet, consisting invariably of a little rice or
barley, mingled with small black beans, to which are added,
according to the season, herbs or wild roots gathered in the
mountains, the whole cooked in water without salt.
"Sometimes," writes Just, "meat can be got, but such
meat as it is impossible to eat; for they never kill a beef
here until it is too old to serve as a beast of burden; hence,
one must renounce all thought of attacking this leathery
flesh with his teeth."[1]

[1] This first impression of the young missionary is somewhat of a mistake, meat
that can be eaten not being unknown to the Coreans, but an article of great luxury.
Their tastes, moreover, differ sensibly from ours, for they consider dog-flesh delicious, and are astonished at the repugnance of Europeans for it. They have also
quite a variety of vegetables and fruits, but these the missionaries seldom saw.
Indeed, in times of persecution, they were reduced to eating the herbs of the fields.
One of them wrote to his parents that he had already eaten a bunch of ferns. These

How did our solitary occupy himself in the narrow prison to which he was confined? His time was divided between study and prayer. The Corean language presents peculiar difficulties to a European, especially the spoken language, for the inflections of the verb are almost incredible in number, each verb having thirty and even forty different forms of conjugation from which one must select according to circumstances. The rules are extremely complicated, and the forms of expression are so different in speaking to a superior, an equal, an inferior, that long practice alone can give the key. On the other hand, the written characters are simple, contrasting notably with the insupportable richness of the Chinese alphabet, sixteen characters representing all the sounds. Hence their books are easily read. But a knowledge of Chinese is almost as necessary as that of Corean, the use of the former being wide-spread throughout Corea. Mgr. Daveluy, with incredible patience and labor, had succeeded in compiling a dictionary in which the ordinary words of the two idioms were rendered into French. He had also successively established four Corean and one Chinese printing presses, by means of which a great number of Christian books were circulated throughout the country. These inestimable treasures, the fruit of years of labor, perished in the persecution of 1866.

Just ardently applied himself to the study of these languages—an arduous task indeed—sustained by his desire of thereby being enabled the sooner to enter upon mission work. He felt keenly his inability to assist his elder brethren, who were almost bent to earth beneath their burden. "The work to be done is immense," he writes, "and the number of missionaries far too few. All are worn out and barely able to drag along, a result due both to lack of

privations are what made Just write in a letter to one of his brethren: "On the missions one has little need of seeking to practise mortifications; they throng upon him from all sides."

proper nourishment and excessive fatigue, the latter especially. At the present time, out of six missionaries capable of working five are sick and almost exhausted; yet they must struggle against these odds, and endeavor to perform their duties as if in health. Of our two venerable Bishops, the one, Mgr. Daveluy, keeps up only by the help of Corean medicines; the other, Mgr. Berneux, has been well-nigh worn out by a fever of five months' standing; nevertheless he does more work than a simple missionary. He has to be carried to the beds of the sick to administer the sacraments to them; and he is not able to perform a baptismal ceremony without sitting down several times. Administrative affairs consuming a great part of the night, one can well understand how excessive must be his fatigue; and truly we are forced to acknowledge the intervention of the good God, without which it would be impossible to sustain such a life any length of time. But no one complains; far from it, for this same good God blesses the missionary's labors in proportion to his trials and sufferings. Many envy the lot of the missionaries in Corea, and it would be still more envied if better known. Happy indeed are they whom God's voice calls to this portion of His vineyard. If not slack in responding to grace, it takes a very little while for them to sanctify themselves here."

We perceive from the above that the pre-occupations of study did not turn Just's soul from the grand object which had attracted it. Love for Jesus Christ animating a faithful heart to sacrifice was ever before his eyes, as the one dominating thought of his life. He even reproached himself for the distractions of soul incident to his long journey by sea and land; he wrote to his young confrères in Paris, advising them to profit by the last months of exterior recollection now left them: he congratulated himself at finding in his forced seclusion leisure for prayer; he sought to imitate the sublime example of interior virtues which he discovered in his venerable Bishop; he studied with admiration the heroic annals of the Church in Corea; he wrote to various religious in Europe, proposing to exchange merits and prayers with them; he interested himself from afar in the foundation of a Carmel at Dijon, hoping that the daughters of St. Teresa would be willing to offer in common their supplications and sacrifices with those of the apostles of Corea; he charged his parents to solicit everywhere prayers for the country of his adoption; in fine, he kept up with some of his old confrères, then missionaries in Thibet, China, Siam, that spiritual correspondence which had been a great delight to him at the seminary, and which now, in the depths of his forced seclusion, reanimated within his soul the fire of holy desires.

"I taste here," he writes to one of them, "the tranquillity of the seminary; and I consider it a most precious favor to be able to pass yet a few more months in this manner. After this I must unite in my life both that of Martha and Mary; nor will the work be wanting. I know missionaries here who keep united to Our Lord amid all their labors. This is very encouraging to me.

"I have recently seen Father Calais. He is exceedingly gentle; and, moreover, he is, according to the expression of Mgr. de Capse, *in the good God's favor*. Notwithstanding his poor health, he accomplishes much good, doing the work of our strongest missionaries.

"I see that any one who desires it may here always find time for prayer and meditation; and yet this mission yields perhaps to none as regards the amount of labor, since the day does not suffice therefor, and one must often work a part of the night, or even the whole night. It is true that some of the spiritual aids which God gives those who live retired in convents are lacking in the most of the missions; but these latter will supply better, perhaps, than anything else motives exciting the soul to a life of faith. This I scarcely realize as yet, but all those who have had experience tell me it is so.

" The study of the language is truly an obstacle to recollection.   It so pre-occupies the mind, returning to it time and again when one wishes to be disengaged from everything.   How weak and miserable is our poor nature ! But Our Lord sees the least exercise of that good will which He Himself puts in our hearts, and whatever one does, provided he often renew the resolution to act for love of God, will suffice.

" The want most felt here is that of the presence of the Blessed Sacrament.   Oh! if I could, like St. Teresa, always see Our Lord with the eyes of faith, present in the depth of my heart, how consoling to me it would be ! But I am so inconstant!

" Pray much for me, a poor sinner, that I may unceasingly raise myself towards Jesus."

Toward his parents his language is that of filial tenderness; but he forgets not to mingle therewith the accents of an apostolic soul, jealous of the spiritual progress of those whom it loves.   He must indeed have had a very high idea of the virtue of his holy parents, to use such vigorous language toward them; it is true, to be sure, that he had never understood in the logic of renunciation how to stop midway. We give below a quotation from the last letter which he wrote them.   It is dated the 5th of November, 1865.

" Adieu, then," he says in termination, " until next year, when I hope to send you tidings of myself again, unless something should occur to prevent it.   I hope that the coming year will bring you many graces, and that you will accept trials from the hand of God with no less thankfulness than consolations.   The good God may probably give

you oftenest what in this life are called troubles and trials;
but he whose heart is fixed not upon the world, but upon
Jesus Christ, calls them jewels added to his crown. Do
not take it unkindly, dear parents, if I wish you as many
of them as the good God will give you strength to bear.
One day you will certainly view this desire as I now do.
But, in a word, may God's holy will be done! The days of
our life here below, spent in sorrow and tears, are so few
compared to those of eternity, that we should rejoice at
having it in our power to merit such happiness by trials so
short and fleeting. Is it not thus we should view these
things? I hope also that you constantly seek more and
more in the holy Eucharist the strength and courage to live
a truly Christian life. *Venite ad me, omnes qui laboratis et
onerati estis, et ego reficiam vos.* Let us not forget these
words."

The memory of our pious missionary again brings before him those works of charity and zeal which filled his
parents' lives. He encourages them therein, and also recommends to their care several poor children in Paris, in
whom he was interested. "Please look after them," he
writes, "although you have others that claim your sympathy and attention, for it is a good work. We must do
like the saints, who when they had nothing else to give
gave their clothing. Tell me something about the churches
you are having built; where are they? Where is St. John's
and where St. Chantal's? Ah! if it were only possible for
us to build churches in Corea! At present there is not
even a chapel here. A room in a Christian house is all the
church (a transient one at that) the missionary has.
Oh! what a contrast with the churches of Europe with
their stately ceremonies and sacred chants! Here Mass
must be said in a half whisper, and not even a *Kyrie eleison*
may be chanted; everything must be done so quietly and

stealthily. I cannot help thinking that when we reach
heaven our singing there will in consequence be louder
than all the rest. Meanwhile we chant in our hearts
thanksgivings for the blessings which divine Providence
unceasingly showers upon us.

"May the grace of Our Lord be ever with you, dear
parents, and daily increase the number of your virtues!
Pray for your missionary child, that he too may sanctify
his soul, and that one day we may all be reunited in our
true country! Adieu! I embrace you in Our Lord, and
pray you to bless me."

The above gives us an idea of Just's interior life during
the nine months he spent in Corea up to the time of his
arrest. His application to study, the knowledge he had
acquired in Mantchooria of the Chinese language, and his
rapid progress in the Corean, all tended to advance the
moment of his active participation in missionary duties.
At the end of some months he was able to make himself
understood by the Christians already accustomed to the
broken speech of the missionaries. Mgr. Berneux now assigned him the final instruction of catechumens and the
administration of baptism. When the Vicar Apostolic had
to be away, Just filled his place in the house, and responded in his stead to the wants of the faithful. In the
last months of 1865 and the beginning of 1866, he heard
from sixty to eighty confessions, baptized at least forty
adults, blessed several marriages, gave confirmation [1] several
times, and administered extreme unction to a number of
sick persons. Almost constantly confined to the dwelling
in which he concealed himself, obliged to practise restraint
in everything, even in his manner of coughing or of blow-

[1] The administration of this sacrament reserved to bishops may, in virtue of a
special delegation of the Holy See, be confided to one who is simply a priest; and in
missionary countries the Vicar Apostolic has the power of transmitting it by this
authority.

ing his nose, for fear of exciting the attention of the pagans passing by the house, he nevertheless went out, when obliged by Mgr. Berneux's absence, to visit the sick. Disguised in his mourning garb, he even went outside the city two or three times to administer the last sacraments to the dying. But a few more weeks and his Bishop, who had promptly appreciated his great merits, would have found in him a most valuable co-laborer. Such was also the opinion of Mgr. Verrolles, who had seen much of him in Mantchooria, and who later was inconsolable at losing him. "What a perfect man!" he writes. "For him martyrdom is bliss! But oh! what good might he not have accomplished had it pleased God to prolong his life! I always wished to keep him with me; and it is a source of deep regret to me that during my absence he left my mission. I would have prevented his leaving. He was of the number of those whose lives should not have been rashly exposed, for God had prepared him to accomplish great works in His Church."

But God needs no one and His designs are impenetrable. The hour was approaching when such noble promises were to be mown down whilst yet in blossom.

We left our Corean Christians a prey to great anxiety, in consequence of the change of rulers. To the regency of the queen was joined that of a mandarin—a most cruel, ferocious man, dreaded by the pagans themselves on account of his tyranny. He had resolved to have the king's palace reconstructed on a grand scale. According to Oriental usage, he understood well how to make the expense of these works fall on the subjects, and even turn to his own profit. Hence the unprecedented exactions, the imposts levied throughout the kingdom, the *voluntary* gifts from rich and poor, both according to their means and beyond them. Resistance meant death. One of the learned men among them believing that his high rank and influence might have some effect upon the regent, addressed him a respectful letter of expostulation, representing to him the probably sad consequences of such abuse of power: it was the executioner who brought the answer.

At this time the tyrant seemed to take no thought of the Christians, and they persuaded themselves that they had nothing to fear. Indeed, some of their number were even on the point of going to the palace to ask why they had not yet been accorded liberty to practise their religion; and they would have carried their design into execution had not the Vicar Apostolic restrained them. Never had this poor people been better disposed. One of Just's letters relates the following touching incident. Two catechumens living in the same province had finished their course of instruction. One of them said to the other, " Now we must go to Séoul to be baptized by the great Bishop."—" But," answered his companion, " what will become of our rice? it will dry up during our absence."— " What! " replied the first, "do you care more for eating rice than for securing your salvation? What matters it if the body die? But if you are not baptized, where will your soul go at death?"—" True, you are right," was the answer. And these two good young men took a long journey of a hundred and twenty leagues to receive baptism.

Mgr. Berneux, whilst admiring the faith of these heroic children, did not share their confidence; and when they spoke to him of the regent's silence, in face of the well-known progress of the Christian religion, he answered: " It is the sleep of the tiger; but the merest accident may awaken him and excite his rage." This accidental occasion, brought about by an incident of foreign politics, was not long wanting.

For several years past the Russians had made such continuous progress in Tartary as greatly alarmed the Corean government for its own independence. Annexion followed annexion, until the Russians were very near the western frontiers of Corea, and touched upon the little river which forms the boundary of the province of Ham-Kieng. [1] In January, 1866, a Russian vessel entered the port of Ouen-San, on the Sea of Japan, and dispatched the Corean Government a peremptory letter demanding that its ports be open to Russian vessels, and that Russian merchants be allowed to establish themselves in the country.

Great consternation was spread throughout the court, and indeed throughout the whole kingdom; and the untoward zeal of a few Christians turned the prevailing wind of agitation against the Church. Convinced that the proceedings of Russia would finally result in religious emancipation, they wrote to the regent, endeavoring to persuade him that the only means of holding the Muscovites at bay was to contract an alliance with France and England, and that the proper person to negotiate this alliance was naturally the Christian Bishop.

The regent received the letter, but expressed no opinion. Did he share the views of those who wrote it? It might be supposed so, since he informed himself of Mgr. Berneux's whereabouts, and expressed a desire to speak with him. The latter had just left Séoul to begin the rounds of his episcopal visitations. Never had his apostolic works been as fruitful. In this one tour of visitations so tragically interrupted, he had baptized with his own hand eight hundred adults. The regent's invitation was sent him and he hastened to comply with it. Four days later, January 25th, he was in Séoul. But the regent, although informed of his arrival, neglected to send for him·

[1] These historic details are borrowed from the accounts of the missionaries who escaped the massacre of 1866, MM. Ridel, Calais, and Féron. They got them from the mouths of the native Christians, witnesses of the events.

and this of itself was sufficient to excite a terrible doubt as to his real intentions. In the interval, it is true, he had had with one of the authors of the letter a long conversation upon the Christian religion; and he professed to admire its morality, but complained of the interdiction upon sacrifices to ancestors. In reality, the regent was gaining time; he wished to be guided by events. All the members of the ministry were bitter enemies of Christianity. Had the exterior peril become more imminent, perhaps the influence of the regent might have been exerted to induce their consent to a plan confiding the safety of the empire to the missionaries. Unfortunately, however, the menaces of Europeans had again proved vain: the Russian vessel withdrew, and intolerance and cruelty triumphed. The Coreans now recalled the groundless fears with which they had been filled at the time of the Anglo-French expedition against China. "These devils of the West," they said, "are to be feared only on the sea; they dare not descend upon our coasts, much less penetrate into our country. Did we not put to death several of their priests, and did they ever offer to avenge it? Since these preachers of impiety have denounced themselves in offering their intervention, it is a good opportunity to exterminate them and thus end their sect."

Such were the designs now being meditated upon at court; and the regent, even supposing his sentiments and views were altogether different, was not the man to expose himself for the protection of the Christians. Measures of injustice and violence were in accordance with his nature. He went with the current, and the missionaries' destruction was resolved upon.

Meanwhile Mgr. Berneux, wearied of uselessly waiting for the regent's summons, had again left Séoul and resumed his apostolic works, but without going far from the capital.

He returned thither in a few days, on the 5th of February. His confidence had begun to increase. A note which he wrote on the 10th of February to M. Féron contains the expression of his hopes. " I do not know," he says, " whether in my last letter I asked you to celebrate a Mass for the peace of the kingdom, and the happy termination of the affairs now occupying all minds. It is the king's mother (but do not tell this) who desires each missionary to offer a Mass for these intentions. . . . Yes, there is a snake in the grass, and it seems in no hurry to come out. I have been awaiting an interview with the regent since he sent me word to return in all haste; I thought it would have taken place ere this, but I have heard nothing more from him. However, we have made a big step towards liberty of conscience. Pray Our Lord and His good Mother to aid me in these grave matters. Also advise the Christians to be very circumspect."

Alas! on the 14th of February, four days after writing the above, the holy Bishop was disabused of all illusion regarding the fate in store for him. Armed minions of the government came to search his house, under the pretext of treasury regulations. Mgr. Berneux saw that they wished to assure themselves of his person, but he believed, at first, that they proposed only to keep him in sight; consequently he would not change his retreat, fearing that if he did so, the police, in order to discover his whereabouts, would search all Christian houses, and the disturbance thus become general.

The treachery of a perfidious Christian, a servant to the Bishop of Capse, brought about what the latter in his devotedness was anxious to avert. This creature betrayed to the government satellites the exact place of abode of the other missionaries, scattered throughout the kingdom, and their arrest was decided upon.

As we are not writing the general history of the persecution of 1866, we shall relate in detail only the facts immediately concerning M. de Bretenières, or those in some
manner connected with him. We will state, however, that
Mgr. Berneux was the first arrested. At four o'clock in
the afternoon of February 23d his house was entered; he was
seized and bound; but making no resistance, he was almost
immediately unbound and conducted, first, to the *right tribunal* (so called because situated to the right of the king's
palace); then to the *Kou-Riou-Kan*, or prison where the
lowest grade of criminals are confined, all mingling together.
But on the morrow, or the next day after that, he was
transferred to the *Keum-Pou*, or prison reserved for the
nobility and state criminals.

In our country, and all others enlightened by the benefi-
cent rays of Christianity, the prison is a place of suffering
only inasmuch as it deprives one of liberty; trials in our
criminal courts have but one end in view—to discover the
true culprit; in fine, the supreme punishment, death, is
inflicted in a manner most rapid and simple. But nations
that have never known the blessed influences of the Gospel
are strangers to everything that savors of the humane in
their punishments. The prison itself is an abode of misery
and suffering; every examination of the accused is accompanied by tortures; and the sentence of death is carried
out in the slowest and most appalling forms.

Corea is no exception to this rule; and to reach the limits of cruelty in their treatment of the disciples of Jesus
Christ, these persecutors of Christianity had but to comply
with the regulations of their criminal code. It is true,
apostasy ordinarily afforded a means of escape; but even
then it rarely happened that the torture was not continued
for a while, either by way of chastisement or to oblige the
sufferer to disclose the names of his accomplices, that is,

his co-religionists. To begin with, the prison itself is a place of torture, the epitome of suffering. It consists of small wooden barracks built up against the walls of a vast enclosure and opening on an inner court. These sheds have no windows, the only opening being a little door. Air and daylight never penetrate them, but in winter the cold, in summer the heat, reign supreme. Lying on the bare ground, soaked by the infiltrations of rain when the weather is bad, the prisoner by turns is stifled or nearly frozen, at the same time breathing an infected air, condemned to live in filth, eaten up by vermin, and a prey to hunger and thirst, for his nourishment consists only of a little porringer of millet, about the size of one's fist, passed in to him twice a day. In the *Kou-Riou-Kan* the sound of a bell continually ringing prevents the captives from communicating with one another, and also disturbs their repose. Confessors of the Faith who have passed through the great persecutions are unanimous in declaring that they dread imprisonment a hundred times more than torture.

And yet what tortures accompany the interrogations! The most common, that which no accused person or criminal escapes, is the bastinado on the legs. Seated in a wooden chair, to which he is securely tied, the accused, at every question addressed to him, receives a certain number of blows on the fore part of his legs, inflicted with cudgels, either square, or triangular, like the legs of some tables. The bones are bruised and often broken.

To this ordinary treatment they add, in graver cases, the bending of the bones, dislocation of them, the torture of the plank, puncture by sticks, suspension, sawing of the bones, etc.

The bending of the bones is accomplished by inserting a piece of wood between the legs, which are secured to the ground by pegs, and gradually forcing the knees to approach until the tibias bend without breaking. The dislocation of the bones consists in tying the arms behind the back, and bending the shoulders backward towards each other: the bones are dislocated and often break.

The puncture by sticks consists in thrusting sharpened sticks into all parts of the body; in the plank torture the criminal is struck sharp blows on the calves of the leg, with the edge of a piece of oak, until the flesh flies in great pieces.

In the torture by suspension, the victim is hung up by the arms, previously bound behind his back; and whilst thus hanging, he is beaten so furiously with rattans that death would surely ensue were he not from time to time let down to get breath. The torture called sawing of the bones is accomplished by passing cords of horsehair around the limbs, and drawing them alternately in opposite directions until they cut into the flesh.

After undergoing one or several of these tortures, the victim receives some little attention, and is taken back to prison to await the next examination. The sentence of death is nearly always preceded by three or four trials of this sort, at intervals of several days. What, indeed, must not be the sufferings of these poor creatures, cast, all bleeding and mangled, upon the bare ground of the prison, there to await new tortures, meanwhile consumed by fever, hunger, thirst, and a prey to all sorts of vermin and insects, penetrating their flesh and engendering corruption in their wounds.

Let us now resume the thread of our narration. On the 23d of February, the day of Mgr. Berneux's arrest, M. de Bretenières had gone to a *kong-so*[1] in Séoul, where he heard two confessions, administered confirmation to one,

_____
[1] *Kong-so* means place of assembly, and is the name given to the house of a Christian, temporarily decorated for the celebration of the offices of the Church or the administration of the sacraments.

and blessed a marriage. On turning home he heard of his Bishop's arrest. Not yet knowing what the result might be, nor what the extent of the persecution, he took no measures whatever, except to send word of it to Mgr. Daveluy and the other missionaries with whose present places of abode he was acquainted. Having done this, he awaited events with that tranquillity which was ever the foundation of his virtue. On the 24th, which was next day, he said Mass for the last time. On the morning of the 25th his house was surrounded, and he, with the catechist, Mark Tieng, arrested. His servant, Paul Phi, was out at the time, and owed his life to this circumstance. The two prisoners were guarded in their dwelling for twenty-four hours, not being taken away until day-break of the 26th. Like Mgr. Berneux, Just offered no resistance, and he was at first treated respectfully, two satellites of the government holding him merely by the sleeves of his robe, and a red cord, reserved for criminals of rank, being tied loosely around his arms, which were crossed upon his breast.

He was treated in all respects just as his Bishop had been. Conducted to the right tribunal, he was first interrogated without torture. Incapable of conversing freely in the Corean tongue, being familiar with only such words and phrases as were needed for the holy ministry, he simply repeated, in answer to the interrogatories, "I came to Corea to save souls; and I will joyfully die for God."

From the tribunal he was conducted to the prison for robbers, the *Kou-Riou-Kan*, a filthy, disgusting place, the door of which, on entering, he opened and shut rapidly several times, doubtless to introduce a little air fitted for respiration.

Next day he was transferred to the *Keum-Pou* prison, reserved for criminals of rank. Here each one has a cell to himself. On the following days he was taken thence to undergo four interrogatories, either before the ministers, or before the chief judges of the right tribunal or the left.

Upon one side of a vast rectangular court is erected the elevated platform of the tribunal. In the middle of the enclosure is the accused, bound by the legs and shoulders to a chair, so securely, that even under blows he cannot make the least movement. Around him stand four, six, or eight executioners in two lines, holding the instruments of torture. Behind these, separated from the accused by a curtain, is seated the scribe who notes down his responses. A few steps back of these again, eighty soldiers, armed with divers instruments of torture, are ranged in the form of a horse-shoe, whilst a second line in the rear consists of the usual crowd of the curious. As soon as the examination begins, the eighty soldiers set up a sort of dull, cadenced chant, drowning the voice of the accused, and thus preventing his words or cries from being heard by the public.

But in the crowd are many Christians, religiously attentive to each circumstance of the drama; and it is to their depositions, subsequently received, when the persecution had ceased, that we owe the following details, which unfortunately, however, are incomplete.

In each of the four examinations, Just received the bastinado upon the bones of his legs, the bottom of his feet and his great toes; he also underwent the puncture of sticks. Perhaps, like the Bishop of Capse, he endured other tortures, but there is no testimony to that effect.

The witnesses are unanimous in declaring that next to Mgr. Berneux, the principal object of their pagan persecutors' hatred, no one was more cruelly tortured than Just. His imperfect knowledge of the language forced him to a silence, broken only by his profession of Faith. No less vain than cruel, the judges regarded this silence as an insult to the tribunal. Moreover, the young missionary, before his arrest, had resided near his Bishop, which fact probably giving the impression that he had a sort of pre-eminence over the others, was of itself sufficient to single him out for the greatest severities.

During all his tortures, the Christians remarked that this angelic young man uttered no cry; not even a sigh escaped his breast. With eyes modestly cast down and countenance unmoved, the motion of his lips alone revealed the continuity of his prayer. Like the illustrious martyrs of the first ages, he had placed all his confidence in God, and recommended to Him the issue of this glorious combat. *Lætissime et glorianter ibat ad carcerem, quasi ad epulas invitata; et agonem suum Domino precibus commendabat.*[1]

In the exercise of this tranquil heroism, Just proved himself a worthy rival of his holy Bishop, of whom a witness of his tortures remarked, "Mgr. Berneux is always and everywhere full of dignity and sanctity."

After each interrogatory Just's mangled limbs were wrapped in oiled paper, and he was taken back to prison.

When the examinations were ended, the confessors of the Faith were transferred from the *Keum-Pou* to the prison of robbers, the *Kou-Riou-Kan.* Here their hardships were much greater than in the former place; but they had the supreme consolation of being able to communicate with each other.

Who shall tell us of what passed between this holy Bishop and his priest in these last meetings, sublime vigils of martyrdom? St. Sixtus and St. Lawrence, had they been allowed to suffer together, would probably have exchanged no words save such as now fell from the lips of these two.

MM. Beaulieu and Dorie were arrested on the 27th and 28th of February, in a province a little distance from

---

[1] Office of St. Agnes, anthem of II. nocturn, Roman Breviary, February 5th.

Séoul.   Taken to the city, they were subjected to the same interrogatories and shared the fate of the Vicar Apostolic and his companion.

The last examination was terminated for each of them by the sentence of death.   Several days elapsed before the execution—days passed amid the tortures of a wounded, mangled body, and the sufferings of a captivity more cruel still, but also—and we cannot doubt it, for the joy depicted on the faces of each victim at the hour of immolation is proof undeniable—amid the holy ecstacies of hope and love.

On the 8th of March, 1866, the four condemned men were taken from prison, Mgr. Berneux first, then MM. de Bretenières. Beaulieu and Dorie, immediately after their head and their father.   Unable to stand, they were each carried in a long wooden chair, their legs and arms extended forward and bound to the bars, their heads drawn backward and tied to the back of the chair by the hair. Above the head of each, even as above our Saviour's cross, was a small tablet bearing the following inscription: "———(here was inserted the Corean name of the missionary),[1] a rebel and contumacious, condemned to death after having undergone torture several times."

During the passage from the prison to the place of execution, the bearers rested several times; and Mgr. Berneux took advantage of these intervals to converse with his spiritual sons who were unable to restrain their joy. Sometimes, casting his eyes upon the crowd attracted by curiosity, he would exclaim with a sigh, "Alas! my God! how they are to be pitied."   Some of the assistants having been so dastardly as to insult and jeer at the martyrs, the holy Bishop, and apostle to the end, rebuked them in a tone of firmness.   "Do not laugh and mock at us thus," said he;

[1] Paik was M. de Bretenières' Corean name.

"you should rather weep. We came hither to show you the way to heaven, and behold you have prevented our doing so any longer. How you are to be pitied!"

Capital executions take place in various localities according to the character of the accusation and the rank of the condemned. State criminals are decapitated in a large sandy plain called *Sai-nam-to*, situated fully a league from Séoul, and about ten minutes' walk from the river. The putting them to death is accompanied by the most solemn ceremony and display, all of which only prolongs the victim's agony and sufferings.

On one side of the enclosure is erected a tent for the mandarin who presides at the execution. Besides the military escort accompanying him, are four hundred armed soldiers to hold the crowd in awe.

Mgr. Berneux is the first summoned. Setting on the ground the wooden chair in which he has been carried to the place of execution, the attendants unbind his limbs and strip him of his clothing. They now throw water on his face, which is immediately sprinkled with lime; each ear bent forward over itself is pierced with a dart, which remains fixed upright in the wound. Under the martyr's arms, tied behind his back, they pass a long stick; two soldiers raising him up by this, and holding him in this painful posture, march thus with him around the arena eight times, making the circle they describe less at every turn, so as to end in the middle. A long procession of soldiers, armed with instruments of torture, accompanies the victim. Meanwhile the rest of the military detachment executes marches and countermarches, which display is a diverting spectacle to the crowd. Arrived in the middle of the arena, they placed the holy Bishop on the ground, supported on his knees, his head bent forward, his hair tied with a cord which is held by a soldier. Around him six executioners,

armed with immense, broad-bladed knives, await the signal
for execution. The mandarin gives it, and they immediately begin to dance around the victim, brandishing their
knives, and uttering ferocious cries. Each one is free to
strike just when he chooses, and this cruel sport places at
their mercy the victim's last hours.

At the third blow Mgr. Berneux's head rolls to the
ground, and all the soldiers cry out in one voice, "*It is
done.*" The martyr's head is now picked up and placed on
a small board, bearing also two sticks with which the mandarin can turn the bloody trophy without touching it.
The mournful ceremony is not yet finished; and whilst the
three other missionaries await their fate, the soldiers resume, in inverted order, their spiral march. Having made
the circuit of the arena eight times, they stop before the
tent of the mandarin, and present him the head all dripping
with gore. Then, returning to the place of execution, they
suspend it by the hair to a post, above the body.

Just de Bretenières is the second to pass through this long
course of agonizing cruelty. His smiling serenity never
forsakes him an instant. Ah! this is the hour for which
he has so long and so ardently sighed! He arrives at the
place of execution even as the weary voyager at the welcome port. His head is severed from the body only at the
fourth blow. MM. Beaulieu and Dorie follow him in turn,
undergoing the same tortures. Here also on the 11th of
March, three days later, MM. Pourthié and Petitnicolas,
arrested on the 2d of March, in a neighboring province,
yield up their souls to God after rendering the same testimony to Jesus Christ. With them perished a young Corean,
aged twenty-one, Alexis Ou, who had much to endure in
embracing Christianity, and who proved himself heroic
amidst the most frightful tortures; also a catechist, sev-
enty-three years old, Mark Tieng, a faithful servant of the

missionaries, whose constancy in his last moments was not
less admirable. The death of these eight confessors of the
Faith ended the first act of that bloody tragedy which was
to rob the Church in Corea of so many other precious lives.

According to Corean law, the bodies of criminals must
remain exposed three days in the place of execution; after
which their relatives or friends are at liberty to claim and
bury their remains. At any other time the Christians of
Séoul would not have hesitated to render this pious duty to
their fathers in the Faith. But the terrors of persecution now
restrained them; and according to the customs of the country, it devolved upon the pagans of the neighboring province to provide sepulture. The four martyred missionaries
were interred in one grave. Five months afterwards, there
being a lull in the storm of persecution, the Christians exhumed these blessed remains. Ruined and despoiled of
everything, these poor people could only with the greatest
difficulty find means to defray the very moderate expenses
of these funerals. To procure the four coffins and some
other articles that were necessary, they sold whatever was
still in their possession, one woman selling even her wed-
ding-ring.

At the appointed time, forty of them repaired to the spot
at night, identified the bodies and prepared them all for
burial. The approach of dawn obliged them to withdraw.
Two nights afterwards they returned with holy water and
the books containing the office for the dead. They dug
three large graves. In the first were deposited the coffins of Mgr. Berneux, M. de Bretenières, and Alexis Ou, the
former resting in the centre, with M. de Bretenières at his
right hand, and Alexis Ou at his left. In the second grave
were placed the remains of MM. Pourthié and Petitnicolas;
in the third, those of MM. Beaulieu and Dorie. An earthern
slab at the head of each coffin is inscribed with the mar-

tyr's name. These sacred remains are interred on the side
of a mountain called Ouai-Ko-Kai, about half a league
from Séoul.

Our task is finished; yet ere turning our eyes towards
France, where these mournful tidings will cause so many
tears to flow, we must give our reader a short sketch of
events following the death of the first victims—events
which add such glorious pages to the heroic annals of Corean
Christianity.

CHAPTER VII.

END OF THE PERSECUTION OF 1866.—INTERVENTION OF FRANCE.—NEW TRIALS OF CHRISTIANITY IN COREA (1866–1878).

INFORMED by the traitor Ni-son-i, who betrayed Mgr. Berneux, the mandarins knew that there were still other
French priests in Corea; they also knew their usual place of
abode. The satellites, a sort of armed police or agents
of the military police, were sent out in every direction.
Mgr. Daveluy was the first they apprehended. Summoned
by the regent, he had left Séoul, after waiting vainly for
further orders, and it was whilst on his round of episcopal
administrations that he received M. de Breteniéres' message informing him of Mgr. Berneux's arrest. He at first
considered it a matter of no consequence, and merely summoned MM. Aumaitre and Huin to come to him that they
might confer together on the subject, after which they
separated again. On the 11th of March, the day on which
MM. Pourthié and Petitnicolas were martyred, Mgr.
Daveluy was arrested at the house of a catechist who had

concealed him. Still believing that the government men-aced only the European missionaries, and that there was no danger whatever of a general persecution, he feared that in allowing the search for themselves to be prolonged num-berless Christians might thus be compromised who would otherwise incur no risks; and he sent word to M. Huin to come to join him. The satellites, in expediting the letter, promised Mgr. Daveluy to make no other arrests, but the promise was not kept, and the whole country was soon filled with terror. M. Huin immediately complied with his Bishop's wishes, as did also M. Aumaitre, who had re-ceived the same notice. Influenced by the one charitable thought of shielding the poor Coreans, they both delivered themselves up to the satellites. The rigorous measures taken by these military agents against the missionaries es-pecially sought after left them no hope of escape, even had they so desired; and their concealment for a few days longer would have resulted only in bringing misfortunes and trouble upon numberless other Christian houses already suspected.

Satisfied with this voluntary surrender, the satellites set at liberty those Christians who had been arrested with the Bishop. His servant, Luke Hoang, refused to avail himself of it, declaring that he would share his master's fate. Here, as elsewhere, were seen, side by side, examples of the most sublime devotion and of the blackest perfidy.

As these confessors of the Faith were being conducted to the capital, a rich pagan approached Mgr. Daveluy and said to him in accents of respectful sympathy: " Considered in regard to your soul, what you do is very beautiful; but your fate is terrible and excites my deepest compassion." The Bishop, touched by this expression of generous senti-ment, pressed the stranger's hand in token of gratitude.

Arrived in Séoul and imprisoned in the Kou-Riou-Kan,

the four prisoners underwent the usual interrogatories, accompanied by tortures, the details of which, to our regret, we are not able to give. We do know, however, that Mgr. Daveluy was most cruelly tortured, and also that upon being questioned as to his religion he took advantage of the occasion to deliver a sermon, unfolding the truths of Christianity.

Whilst preparations were being made to have the execution at Sai-Nam-To, a superior order decreed that it take place in one of the provinces. The king being sick, it was necessary to consult the soothsayers, and the execution of the foreigners might have affected the auguries. At the last moment a catechist, Joseph Giang, was added to the four other victims. The five condemned men were taken to Sourieng, upon the sea-coast. The journey was made on horseback, as they were not able even to stand. Their faces, whilst bearing marks of the horrible sufferings the confessors had undergone, were also radiant with that celestial joy which filled their souls. On Holy Thursday, March 29th, as they drew nigh to the place of execution, Mgr. Daveluy heard the satellites talking among themselves, and making arrangements to delay the immolation, in order to display the victims in a neighboring town. Touched by the holy desire of dying on the day which commemorates Our Saviour's death, he cried out in a tone of authority: " What you propose is impossible; we must die to-morrow." God inclined these barbarians to accord the martyrs' desires, and the next day, Good Friday, March 30, 1866, the Bishop of Acones, and his two priests, his catechist and his servant, rendered to Jesus Christ their testimony of blood.

It is said that the mandarin presiding at the execution ordered the martyrs to prostrate themselves before him. It is the custom in Corea for condemned criminals to salute those who sentence them to death. Mgr. Daveluy answered with dignity that he would salute him in the French manner, and refused to go on his knees. A brutal knock threw him face forward on the ground.

Another incident most horrible to think of signalized the holy Bishop's death. The executioner had set no price upon his bloody deed. After a first stroke, which inflicted a terrible gash on the victim's neck, he suddenly stopped, and refused to continue except upon promise of a large sum. The avarice of the mandarin resisted his claim and it was necessary to assemble the officers of the prefecture to decide the case. The discussion lasted a quarter of an hour, the victim meanwhile struggling on the ground in agonizing convulsions. Finally, the bargain was concluded, and two new strokes delivered the martyr's soul.

MM. Aumaitre and Huin and, lastly, the two Coreans were decapitated in turn.

The martyrs' bodies, first exposed for three days, then interred by the pagans in the sand, were some weeks later exhumed by the Christians, and buried in one large grave near a village of the Hong San district.

The hopes of the holy victims who had believed they could save the Corean Christians by sacrificing themselves were cruelly deceived. The persecution spread, and was on a wider scale and of a more ferocious character than any that had ever preceded it. The year of 1866 witnessed scenes of massacre, pillage, devastation. The Christians were ferreted out everywhere, arrested in bands, sometimes put to the most frightful tortures and executed solemnly, sometimes strangled secretly in their prisons. Deprived of the spiritual aid of the missionaries, seeing the ruin of their Church without hope of deliverance, many sought in exterior apostasy a protection which often failed them;

for the hatred of the persecutors seemed more jealous of exterminating Christians than of inducing them to embrace the national belief. The headsman's sabre and the strangler's cord not doing their work quick enough to satisfy the rapacity of the mandarins, they devised a sort of wooden guillotine, which by means of a long beam suddenly let fall upon the necks of the condemned, tied together, could put to death twenty or twenty-five persons at a time. They even went so far as to bury the prisoners alive in great ditches, the earth and stones cast in upon them serving both to cause their death and to afford sepulture to their remains.

Another characteristic of the persecution begun in 1866 was its duration: for four years it continued its work of destruction, with short intervals of peace, followed by fresh outbursts of violence. In 1870 it was estimated that *eight thousand* persons had been put to death during this persecution, to say nothing of those who had succumbed to hardships and hunger. If there be any exaggeration in these figures, it being almost impossible to give the exact statement, we can, at least, say in all truth that the number of victims was immense, and that the whole kingdom was covered with blood and ruins.

The inefficient intervention of the French marine was one of the causes which contributed to the atrocity of the persecution. Informed of the death of the French missionaries, Rear Admiral Roze, who commanded the naval division in the China seas, made, in the month of September, a first demonstration upon the Corean coasts. He returned in October with one frigate, two corvettes, two advice-boats, and two gun-boats. The first operations were well conducted. Attacking the island of Kang-Hoa, which is the arsenal and rampart of Corea, both citadel and town fell into their hands. They now demanded of the Corean government satisfaction for the murder of French subjects. The heads of the nation, encouraged by the impunity attending their previous outrages, disdained a reply. The Admiral now sent a detachment of a hundred and sixty marines without artillery into the interior of the island. Such a force to face the grand warlike preparations of the enemy was ridiculous, and it was soon brought to a stand before a fortified pagoda, from which the sheltered Coreans could fire upon our men, and have nothing to dread from them in return. After heroic but futile efforts, the detachment was obliged to fall back upon Kang-Hoa, with more than thirty wounded, holding in check the Corean soldiers sent in pursuit of them. It had been an easy task to repair this little repulse, by entering the Séoul river with a flotilla and bombarding the capital. But the Admiral feared to take too many warlike steps without instructions from his government; and despite all the entreaties of M. Ridel, who was on board the ship, he set sail for China, leaving the persecutors of Christianity more puffed up with pride than ever, by reason of their so called victory.

The English at Hong-Kong triumphed over our impotence, and spoke of taking in hand themselves the cause of civilization; but as Corea offered no commercial advantages, they merely talked a great deal, but did nothing.

Later on, in 1871, an American expedition, following in the wake of the French and the English, was attended with like results. In consequence of some acts of violence committed by the Corean government upon the persons of American citizens—the massacre of shipwrecked sailors, Admiral Rogers descended upon the coasts of Corea with ships and gun-boats. Like Admiral Roze, he made demands of the government which were of no avail ; then, after an ineffectual demonstration, perceiving the affair promised to be of greater magnitude than any one had imagined, he withdrew, without enforcing his measures, leaving the Coreans more insolent in their fancied superiority than ever. When, we ask, will the governments of civilized nations understand that in treating with barbarous peoples they must choose resolutely between peace and war! Armed intervention in behalf of missionaries and Christians is of questionable utility; even the missionaries themselves are not in accord hereupon. Such of them as desire it acknowledge, moreover, that it presents by the side of evident advantage very grave inconveniences and objections. It confirms the pagans in the belief that the apostles of the gospel are emissaries destined to prepare the way for a foreign invasion; hence the preaching of Christianity becomes an act of hostility against the nation, and the native Christians are considered bad citizens, dangerous to the independence of their country.

If the intervention succeed, it assures, beyond a doubt, a certain measure (rarely sufficient, however) of religious liberty to the convert and security to the missionary. But to say nothing of the bad faith of Asiatics who find so many pretexts for escaping the obligations of treaties, we know that the very success of European claims leads, with commercial relations, to a contact most dangerous to the faith of Oriental Christians. The grand instrument of conquest in the hands of our evangelical laborers is the superior morality of the doctrine which they preach; and the admirable examples these heroes of Christianity set their catechumens give efficacy to their words. When, then, in place of these saints the neophytes see Europeans, Christians in name, but without faith or morals, without even respect for the religion of their country and its ministers; when gold and the propagandism of Protestants reveal to them the divisions which schism and heresy have introduced into the unity of the Church, they are shaken in their belief and influenced by the bad example.

And yet, on the other hand, when vast empires like China, or kingdoms like Corea, obstinately intrench themselves behind absurd prejudices, and make the profession of Christianity a crime against the State, one readily understands that the witnesses and victims of such injustice send forth most ardent sighs for that supreme good of which St. Anselm says that " God loves nothing so much in the world," I mean, *the freedom of His Church.*

We perceive from the above that much may be said for and against this question of temporal assistance given or refused the apostolate. But what is incontestably prejudicial, what unites all annoyances, all perils, to the exclusion of any advantage whatever, is the system of half-measures, insufficient demonstrations, acts of intimidation not followed up. And yet this is the spectacle which, one after another, all European nations and America too have presented in their quarrels with Asiatics, whenever a material interest was not the principal matter at stake. This deplorable policy has caused torrents of blood to flow in China, Anam, Tonquin, and above all, in Corea. Heaven grant that an experience so cruelly acquired may at last enlighten those who hold the sword, and teach them not to draw it henceforth until they have determined to do justice ere returning it to the scabbard!

The reader would not pardon us if we bade adieu to Corea without informing him of the fate of the missionaries who escaped the massacre of 1866.

They were three in number, MM. Calais, Feron, and Ridel. Having succeeded in concealing themselves at the price of unheard-of sufferings, each ignorant of the whereabouts or the fate of the others, hourly expecting death, they profited by these days which God had given them to

sustain, both by word and the administration of the sacraments, the few Christians with whom they could now hold
communication. At the end of two months, on the 15th
of May, M. Ridel rejoined M. Féron. A month later
they had news of M. Calais, and could correspond with him.
After considering the matter, they agreed to send one of
their number into China to represent there the state of
affairs in Corea, and to seek aid. M. Féron, who, in virtue
of his being the eldest of them, was thereby entitled to authority over his brethren, designated M. Ridel for this
perilous mission. The latter, braving a thousand dangers,
succeeded at last in reaching the coast and chartering a
bark manned by Christian sailors. With this crew, strangers to navigation on the open seas, and guided only by
the missionary's compass, he made the voyage.

Landing at Tché-Fou on the 7th of July, he went thence
to Tien-Tsin, and acquainted Rear Admiral Roze with all
that had taken place in Corea. A revolt in Lower Cochin
China obliged the latter to retard measures of retalia-
tion against Corea. When he set out on the expedition
in the following September, M. Ridel accompanied him
as interpreter; and, grieved and disappointed, returned with
the flotilla, after the failure of its attempts, in the month
of October.

Meanwhile, the Corean Christians had assisted MM. Féron
and Calais in embarking on a Chinese junk, which took
them to Tché-Fou. Hence there were now no longer any
priests in Corea. The failure of the French expedition,
the increasing fires of persecution, enkindled anew by this
failure, now rendered the situation of Europeans practically
untenable throughout the kingdom.

The three Corean missionaries repaired to Leao Tong, to
labor under the direction of Mgr. Verrolles at Notre Dame
des Neiges, until circumstances would permit them to return

to their own mission. In 1867 M. Calais and in 1869 M.
Ridel attempted to penetrate into Corea, but both, after
many hardships and risks, were forced to return to Mantchooria. Thence M. Ridel went to Rome, during the
Council; and there he was designated by the Holy Father
to succeed to the glorious heritage of Mgr. Berneux. On
the feast of Pentecost, June the 5th, 1870, he received
episcopal consecration in the church of the *Gesu*, from
the hand of Cardinal Bonnechose, assisted by two Vicars
Apostolic, Mgr. Verrolles of Mantchooria and Mgr.
Petitjean of Japan.

The new Vicar Apostolic of Corea must needs wait a
long time for a favorable opportunity of entering as its
Bishop that country which had reaped the first fruits of
his priesthood.

In 1875, five years after his episcopal consecration, he
made, in company with M. Blanc, a fruitless attempt to
enter by sea. A second attempt in 1876 succeeded. MM.
Blanc and Deguette landed and established themselves at
Séoul. M. Ridel, who also had accompanied them with
the intention of remaining in the kingdom, yielded to the
counsels of the other missionaries and the Christians' entreaties urging him to defer the matter yet a while. At
last, in September, 1877, he penetrated secretly into Corea
with two young missionaries, MM. Doucet and Robert.

In the following January, 1878, a courier of the Vicar
Apostolic on his way to China was intercepted, and this
gave the alarm to the Corean police. On the 28th of the
same month Mgr. Ridel was arrested, and imprisoned in
Séoul. He was treated with respect, and although several
times brought before the tribunal for examination, he was
never tortured. It was evident that the government feared
the intervention of France. His captivity lasted five
months, during which time he suffered much from the

horrors of a filthy, infected prison, and the forced society
of robbers. He was witness of the atrocities committed by
the satellites upon the unfortunate creatures imprisoned
with him, seeing several of them dying of hardship and
want or succumbing to torture, whilst others were strangled
before his eyes. Time and again he believed his last hour
had come, and prepared himself for martyrdom. Probably
he would not have escaped the fate of his predecessor, had
not the Chinese government, at the instance of Patenôtre,
the representative of France at the court of Pekin, demanded his release. Corea yielded to the demands of the
Celestial Empire, and Mgr. Ridel was conducted to the
frontiers of Tartary.

There now remained in Corea four missionaries, one of
whom, M. Deguette, was likewise arrested and sent back
to China. The three others continued, at the peril of their
lives, the evangelization of the country.

After three years of expectant waiting and longing, during which time they made one fruitless attempt to enter
Corea, two new missionaries at last succeeded, about the
month of December, 1880. This expedition ended a series
of voyages made by Chinese barks, to be met by appointment on the Corean coasts. On the 18th of March, 1881,
three months later, one of the two newly arrived, M. Liou-
ville, discovered by the satellites, was arrested and kept under guard in his house; but by order of the governor, who
feared a disturbance in consequence of such arrest, he was
set at liberty in three days. After that the missionaries
had no more trouble with the police.

A breath of liberty had indeed begun to be wafted over
this unhappy country. In this same year, 1881, a Corean-
French dictionary, published at Nagazaki, seemed to prepare the way for relations between Corea and France.
Japan, whence this signal of pacific interchange had been

hoisted, obtained the opening of three Corean ports to its people. In 1882 the United States concluded a treaty with Corea, assuring themselves the same advantages. In 1883 it was England's turn, and her treaty of commerce served as a type for the treaties successively signed by Germany, Austria, Russia, Italy. France entered into negotiations with Corea in 1882, but the treaty was not concluded until 1886, and not ratified until 1887. Since June, 1888, a French commissioner resides at Séoul.

Corea is now open to trade and everything bids us hope that, commercial barriers being broken down, freedom of religion will also be guaranteed. However, we must in all cases expect to contend with the strength of inveterate prejudice, and the rancor of those who cannot pardon the evil these prejudices have wrought. Until the year 1886 the missionaries had to live concealed. At the present time they may show themselves in the various ports and at Séoul; but it would not be prudent for them to do so in districts which are far from the capital.

Our zealous missionaries, whom even this most violent persecution did not render inactive, have lost not a moment in profiting by the restoration of peace to Corea.

In 1882 Mgr. Ridel, kept from his mission by sickness, appointed M. Blanc his coadjutor; and the latter repaired to Japan in 1883, to receive episcopal consecration at Nagazaki. He made the two voyages publicly, leaving Corea on a Japanese steamer and returning on a German one.

June 20, 1884, the death of Mgr. Ridel, companion of the martyrs and confessor of the Faith, passed over to Mgr. Blanc the title and office of Vicar Apostolic.

The new head of the Corean Church immediately put his hand to the work. In the month of September he secretly collected at Séoul his eight missionaries in order to enter upon a spiritual retreat with them, hold a synod,

make a new division of the districts and take various measures corresponding to the new state of things.

Since that time each portion of the Vicariate has been
annually visited and administered to by him.

Charity follows close upon Faith, walking in her footsteps. In 1885 Séoul saw this exemplified in the form of
an orphan asylum of the Holy Infancy and a home for the
aged. These two establishments, at first in charge of native Christians, were a few months ago (July, 1888)
confided to the care of four Sisters of St. Paul of Chartres. Several hundred children and numberless old people
have already been received.

Finally, we mention the commencement of the construction of the first Christian church in Séoul—a thing
deemed impossible until very recently,

At the present time a Vicar Apostolic and thirteen missionaries evangelize Corea. The Christian population numbers over 20,000, and conversions are multiplying. After a century of unparalleled sufferings, the poor Corean
Church, whose annals we have just given, sees, at last.
Christian civilization prevail over barbarism. This blessed
result is the work of God; but it is permitted us to dis-
tinguish therein two visible agents—the heroic constancy
of the native Christians and the apostolate of France.
Whilst there are those who would rob our dear country of
her Faith and worship, it is she who plants the cross upon
Corea's inhospitable shores, the blood of her missionaries
that waters it, and the charity of her consecrated virgins
that replaces the horrors of barbarian cruelty by the sublime tenderness of compassion.

The young martyr, the story of whose holy life and
glorious death we have narrated, had his share in this
supernatural fruitfulness. It was destined to praise him,
and to show *Christian peace* flourishing over his tomb. If

we have allowed the series of events connected with our subject to take us too far from the main path and consume too much of our time, the reader will pardon us, we know, when he remembers that the dying missionary's vision embraced this future, that his last mortal supplications invoked it, and that he offered himself in sacrifice to hasten its coming.

But we must bear in mind that our task is not that of a historian but of a biographer. Hence we return to that fatal moment which beheld the headsman's glittering blade sever from their bodies the heads of these holy victims of the persecution of 1866; and we follow in thought the mournful message bearing to Just de Bretenières' parents the news of their son's death.

CHAPTER VIII.

JUST'S MARTYRDOM IS MADE KNOWN TO HIS PARENTS.—
SOLEMN COMMEMORATION OF HIS MARTYRDOM AT DIJON,
MARCH 8, 1867.—LAST SOUVENIRS (1866-1867).

THE events which took place in Corea March, 1866, were known in France in the early part of the following September. From the latter days of August, M. and Mme. de Bretenières were filled with anguish, having learned through dispatches to the English journals of the massacres in Corea. On the 5th of September M. Albrand, Superior of the Society of Foreign Missions, confirmed the sad news, in a letter which he wrote to the Bishop of Dijon, at the same time enclosing therein the following letter to M. de Bretenières—a letter which is indeed a model of Christian simplicity, delicacy, and sublimity. He says:

" MOST HONORED SIR:—I can to-day address you thus

with more truth than ever. Yesterday we received news direct from our dear Corea—news grave and memorable, which the annals of the holy Church will ever hold in remembrance. God's designs are impenetrable to our feeble understandings, but Faith teaches us that His divine providence permits nothing that is not finally directed to the salvation of the elect. Let us always and everywhere adore this paternal providence of God, and all that happens to us will be for us only a means of sanctification, and a sure guarantee of celestial benedictions.

" The following, most honored Sir, are the details which have reached us of these last occurrences in Corea. Last January some European (Russian) ships appeared on the Corean coast, and demanded of the government the opening to them of a port and a concession of land for commercial purposes. This peremptory summons excited great consternation at court, and throughout the country. As the regent sought a means of settling the matter discreetly, and as he was moreover personally very well disposed towards the Christian religion, certain Christians thought this an excellent opportunity of rendering a service to our holy religion, by bringing it to play a part herein; and they suggested to the regent that the two Corean Bishops and their missionaries might prove valuable intermediaries. Filled with fear, the regent welcomed the proposition and had the two Bishops summoned. Mgr. Berneux, making his round of administrations, and having little confidence in the affair, placed difficulties in the way of his return; but his presence was officially known. He was at length obliged to yield to new summonses from the regent, and repaired to Séoul.

" Meanwhile the Russian vessels had disappeared, and with them the fears of the Corean government. Prominent at court was a party thoroughly hostile to the Christians, and seeing the Bishop in their hands, as it were, they proposed to seize him and all his missionaries. Despite the regent's opposition to this at the beginning, their counsels at last prevailed over him, and Mgr. Berneux was made prisoner. Orders were given at the same time to seize Mgr. Daveluy and nearly all the other missionaries their places of concealment having been made known to the government by a traitor. In the course of the month of March the two bishops and all their missionaries, save three, found themselves in the hands of their persecutors, who, emboldened by this first success and blinded as to the possible consequences of their conduct, carried their cruelties to the utmost. In permitting His enemies this excess of rage, God crowned two Bishops and seven missionaries with the crown of immortality.

"The details are wanting, but we know that on the 8th of last March Mgr. Berneux triumphantly bore off the palm of martyrdom with M. Dorie, M. Beaulieu, and one other of his missionaries. On the 11th of March M. Pourthié and M. Petitnicolas gained the same victory. Finally, on the 30th of the same month, Mgr. Daveluy obtained the crown of martyrdom, in company with M. Aumaitre and M. Huin, at noon, Good Friday, thus renewing in their persons the sacrifice which the divine Redeemer offered for love of us, on the same day and at the same hour, on Mount Calvary.

"We know that these nine confessors of the Faith met their death with a serenity and joy which shone forth in their countenances, happy to quit this vale of tears, and await us in the bosom of God, amid the splendors of eternity.

"I have named to you, most honored Sir, all these venerable martyrs but one—and there the thought of a father's and a mother's heart stopped me. I feel assured that these same hearts will of themselves name him whom I forbore to mention. I now beg pardon for having perhaps not given sufficient weight to those sentiments of faith animating your family, and for hesitating an instant in telling you of the grace it has pleased God to bestow upon you, in placing your beloved son in the choir of martyrs. The very day on which M. Just was seized he had just baptized twenty-five catechumens.[1]

"This, most honored Sir, is the only detail which it is possible for me to give you at present. I earnestly implore the Lord of the apostles and the Queen of martyrs, to soften for you and all your venerable family the grief which poor human nature must feel on such an occasion. Faith will raise you above nature, and you will bless God for the meed of glory which he has deigned to accord your dear child.

"In the charity of Our Lord Jesus Christ, and in the remembrance of our venerated martyr, deign to accept, most honored Sir, for you and yours, my respectful affection and entire devotion.

Delpech."

Charged with the delivery of this sad message, Mgr. Rivet went to the home of the young martyr's parents and acquitted himself of his mission with all the tenderness and delicacy inspired by holy charity. Having prepared them for the news, he gave them the letter which we have just read. The father shed tears abundantly, but the mother did not weep; her mute agony was terrible to behold. The first moments of such a shock over, the pious Bishop had but to suggest it to receive from the lips of these truly grand Christians their expression of perfect resignation; they renewed in his presence the sacrifice they had made to God

---

[1] This detail is a mistake. **The information given in Chapters V. and VI. is more** accurate.

of their child, and even recited with him and their second son the *Te Deum*, in thanksgiving for the glorious privilege accorded him.

Later on, M. and Mme. de Bretenières received letters from the missionaries who had known Just—among others from MM. Calais and Ridel, who had shared with him all the perils preceding the massacre, and barely escaped it. Little by little the details arrived, and from all parts were testimonies rendered to the young apostle's virtue and congratulations addressed to the parents whom God had found worthy of giving the Church a martyr. They to whom these words of Faith were addressed were indeed worthy of them. Their sorrow was unfathomable; the poor mother, whose fortitude at the final parting seemed to surpass her husband's, now felt her heart torn and rent asunder at thoughts of the tortures her beloved child had endured. St. Bernard says that the lance which pierced Our Saviour's side pierced the heart of Mary first. It is the mother's prerogative to suffer, and to feel less keenly her own sufferings than those of her children.

Life had henceforth no charms for these admirable Christians—I was going to say, no motive for existence. Earth presented to their gaze only a subject for tears; but heaven, where Faith showed them in glory and beatitude him whom their eyes would never again behold here, attracted them with ever-increasing force, and became the one desire of their hearts. Their lives, more than ever detached from the world, were ceaseless aspirations towards their eternal home. Whilst their second son pursued his ecclesiastical studies, they passed their winters in Rome, so as to be near him. The remainder of the year was devoted to works of zeal and charity, which had always had so large a share in the employment of their time. And thus in the exercise of these most beautiful, **gentle virtues they** ended their earthly pilgrimage, the **Baron de Bretenières in 1882,** aged seventy-eight years; his **worthy companion in 1886, aged** seventy-nine **years.**

The various birthplaces of the Corean **martyrs** celebrated with religious solemnities the **anniversary of their glorious** death. Amiens distinguished itself **by the grandeur of the** homage there rendered **the memory of Mgr. Daveluy. On** the 8th of **March, 1887, Dijon had also its solemnity, on** which occasion **Mgr. Mermillod, Bishop of Hébron, pro-** nounced in the cathedral of St. Bénigne the funeral ora- tion of the young martyr **who honored his country more** by his glorious death than he **could ever have done by the** most brilliant **worldly career.** Arriving **at Dijon on the** very day of the solemnity, and ignorant of his young hero's history except in a general way, the orator spent the morn- ing in informing himself, through Just's friends, of his principal characteristics; and his words of eloquence, glow- ing with the warmth of emotions awakened by all he had just heard, **rang through the vaults of the old basilica in** tones of **touching pathos.** There still sounds in our ears one passage **of his discourse.** Recalling **with exceeding** delicacy **and** appropriateness the **regret which, amid the** hardships of **his life in Corea, Just expressed for the lack of** becoming accompaniments **to the** celebration **of the** divine mysteries there, in contrast to the pomp and splendid cere- monial **of European worship, all beauty and melody, he** exclaimed, "Young martyr, sing, sing now! It is no longer the *Kyrie* **of sorrow and pain that flows from your** lips, but the *Gloria* of thanksgiving. Nor is it the *Credo,* that symbol **of the Faith,** abiding though obscure, **for which** you poured out your blood—no, it is now the canticle of the undimmed vision and of eternal love."

A letter **to Mme. de** Bretenières **from M. Bon,** mission- **ary to Western** Tonquin, informs her that two of his brethren, through a novena to her martyred son, obtained the conversion of a person who had not been to confession for fifty years.

A still more remarkable fact is the following. A near relative of Just was attacked by an incurable malady. He had been a stranger to the sacraments since his youth, and the loss of an only son had greatly embittered him against Providence. His wife and his daughter unceasingly implored Heaven in his behalf, but apparently in vain. His violent, obstinate temper was such as to make him feared by all around, notwithstanding the deep affection his many admirable qualities inspired. No one dared speak to him of his religious duties for fear of increasing his obstinacy on this point. A timid overture made by his wife, who saw that the disease was gaining upon him, met with a response that discouraged all further attempts. Suddenly, one day, without any one having perceived the slightest sign of a change in his disposition, he calls his wife and tells her to send for the parish priest. He confesses, receives the sacraments, and dies a few days afterwards in the most admirable sentiments. This was in March, 1866. Some months later the afflicted family heard the news of Just's death, and found that the dying man's sudden conversion had taken place just a few days after the martyrdom of the nephew whom he had always so tenderly loved. Just returned his affection, and had never ceased to pray for him. The boon which in life he had never been able to obtain from Heaven was granted him through martyrdom.

Let us now finish this collection of souvenirs by the narration of a little incident, which, while not attributing to it anything of a miraculous character, we cannot but regard as certainly a touching and graceful symbol.

One day, at Dijon, when Just was about nine or ten years old, he planted a rose-bush in the yard of the Sisters of St.

Vincent de Paul, belonging to the parish of Notre Dame. Rose-bushes are very long-lived. Twenty years afterwards this rose-bush was still living, but, astonishing to say, it had never bloomed, and several times the gardener, like the master of the vineyard mentioned in the Gospel, wished to dig up the sterile plant. But the Sisters, cherishing it as a memento of the young missionary, forbade him. Suddenly, in the spring of 1866, for the first time it put forth buds —four buds which gradually expanded into four beautiful roses. It was just about the period when, transplanted from Corea's inhospitable shores, the young martyr's soul blossomed into unfading beauty amid the flowers of heaven. The rose-bush still lives, and since then has never ceased to bloom.

THE END.

PRINTED BY BENZIGER BROTHERS, NEW YORK.

www.ingramcontent.com/pod-product-compliance
Lightning Source LLC
Chambersburg PA
CBHW030551040726
47497CB00008B/2676